VAGABOND

VAGABOND

by
A.P. Wolf

FOURTH ESTATE · *London*

First published in Great Britain in 1991 by
Fourth Estate Limited
289 Westbourne Grove
London W11 2QA

A catalogue record for this book is
available from the British Library

ISBN 1-872180-18-3

Typeset in Erhardt by York House Typographic Ltd, Hanwell, W7
Printed and bound by Cox & Wyman Ltd, Reading

1

I am sitting on the twenty-fourth storey of a hotel in Singapore.

I am having a very serious nervous breakdown.

I am too frightened to leave the room.

When the room service people bring my drinks and food I hide in the toilet. I make them push the bill under the toilet door for me to sign. I think that at any moment a Singapore Airlines 747 is going to come homing in for Changi Airport, make a slight, unscheduled detour and end up embedding itself in my hotel room. I think that if there is a fire I will die. I can't run down twenty-four flights of stairs quicker than a fire. Anyway, what if the fire starts on the ground floor?

I've been drunk now for . . . I've forgotten how many days. No hangovers though. When I wake up from my nightly hour's sleep – and I only get that one hour by drinking myself into a total coma – I just drink again. When I feel sober, I drink twice as much; if I'm sick, I drink more to take the taste away again. I really think this is IT, this is the big one, I'm going to die right here in this shitty little hotel room. The phone rang once so I poured a bottle of gin over it, but it kept on ringing.

I want to be alone, but even here in this block of concrete isolation people are disturbing me. Every half an hour or so someone slips cards under my door. They are for massage services. 'Sexy young girls' will do certain things to me, for a certain price, in the comfort and privacy of my hotel room.

1

'OK, I'm into that,' I decide after a long time when I have collected a hundred of these cards and laid them all out on my dirty bed and studied the pictures of pretty Oriental girls posing in what I assume to be the normal pose of a sexy young female massage person. In an attempt to get myself back to reality I will give it a go. I call the hotel manager. I find I can still just about function as a human being on the telephone, even though it is all sticky and stinks of gin.

'What are these cards?' I ask.

'What cards?' he asks back.

I read them to him:

'We provide a more relaxing massage by qualified and lovely EMI presentable masseuses. Tel: 3381762.'

'Alisan Health Services offer you a satisfying massage. Our beautiful and qualified masseuses will call on you. Telephone 7854345.'

'Sexy Girls Health Service. We provide a younger and charming lady to massage for you. Please call 7580664.'

(These numbers are for real, if anyone feels like a 'massage'.)

'They are for massage services, Sir,' he replies, after a momentary hesitation.

'It sounds like an offer of sex to me,' I tell him. He sounds Japanese. I'm not even going to think about a Japanese hotel manager in Singapore. They are all foreigners here.

'I assure you . . . '

'Can you assure me that if I invite one of these young ladies up to my room I will not end up with the clap?' I ask.

'The clap . . . ?'

'Yes, the clap, naughty diseases, a dose, testical dysentery, that sort of thing . . . '

'I'm sorry, Sir. I don't quite understand . . . '

I cut him off. I am having a nervous breakdown so I am allowed to be rude to hotel managers.

I dial 7580664: Sexy Girls Health Service. It sounds the most promising.

A girl answers. She has the sort of voice that wants to say 'Have a nice day', but she doesn't say it.

2

'I want a massage,' I tell her.

'What sort of massage would you like, Sir?'

'What sort have you got?' I ask.

'Swedish, French, Oriental and of course the normal massage.'

'I want a Siberian massage.'

There is a pause on the other end of the phone. Finally, 'Er . . . what exactly is a Siberian massage, Sir?'

'It's where two of your young ladies take all their clothes off and then beat the living shit out of me with ice-cubes wrapped up in towels. Can you handle that?'

'Of course, Sir,' she answers as if I had just ordered two burgers with ketchup to go.

'How much will it cost?' I ask.

'Three hundred dollars.'

'OK, make that four of your young ladies then.'

'Are you joking, Sir?'

I decide I am. I can just imagine the hotel manager's face when I call room service and order six buckets of ice and four girls come marching up to my room armed with towels. I hang up.

I've been here, locked in this impersonal chamber up in the sky, for a few days now, enjoying my nervous breakdown. The only contact I have with what is going on outside, in the real world, is the television.

On the television is an advertisement for Singapore Airlines, the ultra-sexist one about Singapore girls being a great way to fly. Jesus! Don't these stupid airlines realise that I couldn't care less if a warthog served my dinner on the flight? All I'm concerned about is that the machine flies and that the man sat up front isn't blasted out of his tiny little skull on acid or something. God, I hate flying. I looked at my passport last night and discovered that I've been on more than a hundred flights in the past year. I used to be OK, but now I am terrified. I think it's another stage in my creeping insanity. During take-off I scream like a stuck pig and the people sat next to me quickly find another seat.

Oh yes, the advert . . . Singapore Airlines girls may be the best in the world on the flight deck, but off it they are anything but charming. Ask one to dance at a disco and you'll see what I mean. They react like someone just gave them 2,000 volts with a cattle prod. And they are never satisfied with their hotel room, or anything else for that matter. They are feared and reviled throughout the world because they always complain about everything and *nothing* is good enough for them. Off duty, any of them would make Genghis Khan a good partner on the dance floor.

The advertisement reminds me of a story from my very recent past about a Singapore Airlines girl. It's not just a story, as I was there when it happened. It was on an over-opulent yacht where everyone was drinking too much champagne and doing the sort of things they shouldn't have been doing. I know they wouldn't have been doing those things if they had known, like me, that everything was being recorded on good quality video cameras concealed behind the ornate mirrors. 'Everyone' is not quite right: the Singapore Airlines crew were being very circumspect – which, if you know anything about most aircrews when they let their hair down, you will know is unusual.

One Singapore Airlines girl was sat next to the Boss – I can't say who or what he is, apart from that he is an Arab gentleman with too much money and power; if I said any more I would earn a very black mark in my copybook and might get to wear one of those nice black plastic suits that zip all the way over the head – trying to resist his attempts to infiltrate her bikini. He was dressed in baggy shorts as usual, and when you saw him like that you really couldn't believe he was who he was. Anyway, the girl turned around to the Boss while she was trying to slap his exploring hands away and said, 'When is the Boss arriving? I only came to meet him, they say he is a funny little man. A real pervert!'

I was sat on the other side of them and had to have on-the-spot hysterics. The Boss did as well. He patted her hand and said, 'When he arrives, I promise to introduce you to him.'

I told her later that she had been sitting next to the Boss the whole time and she ran off and stuck her head in a bucket of champagne for the rest of the night.

The Boss tells that story to everyone, but he doesn't invite

Singapore Airlines crew on the yacht any more. He sticks to what he knows works and invites representatives of two or three of the biggest international airlines. Every stewardess (and a respectable number of the stewards too) who has made the trip wears a gold Rolex or Chopard with those nice little diamonds that sparkle around the edges as a badge of honour in memory of her night on the yacht.

Actually, it's not as simple as that. There is a system and I should set it out to be faithful to the truth.

First visit the girl gets a nice little Baume and Mercier, second time around she graduates to an Omega, third time there is a nice gold Rolex; and for the true professionals – the girls who keep coming back for more and more – there is the gold Chopard studded with all sorts of goodies, plus a pair of diamond earrings and $12,000 thrown in to cover any incidental expenses.

Don't think these watches are giveaways. Those girls work bloody hard for them. I know, I've seen the videos.

So next time you are sat on a plane take a look at the wrist watches and see if you can spot the naughty ones. They are not uncommon on many of the world's favourite airlines.

Shit! I am going insane. I'm giving away company secrets here, and will have to start learning to swim with sharks if I can't keep quiet.

I'll get away from that subject.

On the television news the main story is of an unfortunate youth who got caught short in the elevator and had to take a piss. No sooner had the last drop hit the floor than alarm klaxons screamed out and the elevator came to a dead stop between floors. The elevators in Singapore have urine-detectors. Penalties are severe.

Don't get me wrong. I do not approve of people pissing in elevators, though in the case of journalists I make an exception. But there is something about urine-detectors in elevators that gives me the cold shivers. Perhaps there are video cameras behind my hotel-room mirrors. What a startling record of self-abuse that would provide. Perhaps there are hidden microphones in the hotel bar waiting to catch someone saying that a certain person here in Singapore is not immortal. I met that certain person. He shook my hand at St John's school in Singapore in 1967, so perhaps he really is immortal. Whenever I get into an argument anywhere in the world I always trot that one out. I say, 'Don't mess with me, man. I met Mr Lee Kuan Facking Yew in 1967 and he shook my hand.'

That shuts anybody up. It's like telling people you just met God.

My nervous breakdown. It has a source. A lot of sources, actually, that have all been building up for the last eight years since I started working for the Boss. I guess I must be the only person who ever lasted that long with the Boss. Most of the others were carried off on stretchers or strapped onto an aeroplane clutching a whisky bottle and dribbling down their chins after just two or three years. But it all sort of came together for me a few days ago with a bad bloody experience in Bangkok. Well, I think I had a bad bloody experience in Bangkok. I know I was in Bangkok, that's a certainty, but I'm still not exactly sure what happened. That's the problem with a nervous breakdown, events and time become mixed up, fiction becomes fact and vice versa.

Bangkok is one hell of a place. Conversation is limited in that city. Whatever you want to talk about, the conversation comes around to sex.

The bellboys ask, 'You need a girl, Sir?'

The elevator attendants, instead of asking which floor, want to know if Sir desires a young lady.

The waiters ask, 'What about a nice young girl for you, Sir?' as if they are asking you whether you want some cream in your coffee.

You watch pathetic, overweight European geriatric males running around with sixteen-year-old Thai beauties and you want to throw up in a big bucket and kick them up the arse and tell them that what they are doing is exploiting people who are so damned nice but so damned poor that they don't get any choice and have to lay down on dirty beds and spread their legs while some old fool pumps away at them until a dribble of stuff comes out and satisfies the rich, fat man that he still has it in him and the girl crouches in the bath and washes away the dead fluid that is about as important to her as the latest toothpaste on the market, so you watch it and you watch it and you want to go out and buy an AK47 and you want to start blowing people all the way to China and back again. You want to burst into their hotel rooms and make pretty patterns on the wallpaper with explosive ammunition and take dirty pictures of them and send them in unmarked envelopes back to their comfortable homes and wives in Europe with a note saying, 'Your old man is an animal. He screws girls ten years younger than your daughter.'

But who gives a shit? Everyone is having a good time. You know what I mean? Don't misunderstand me, I'm no saint. I slept with whores. It cost me ten dollars and I got syphilis. It was in New York, the capital of our modern world, and I was all of fifteen years of age . . . It was great. We used to go down to the blood bank, sell a pint of blood for the ten dollars and then go and spend it on a Times Square whore. They used to love my accent, they ate me up and spat me out again. It was just a way of earning a living to them. But at least they weren't part of a national industry. They weren't part of a system that can sell a nine-year-old girl to some so-called civilised white man, and a doctor at that, who then rams a vibrator into her so bad that she ends up in intensive care, requiring extensive surgery. I read that in the paper. The girl cost him three hundred dollars because she was a virgin, and he couldn't get it up. He even took pictures. I'm seriously thinking of spending a grand and having him rubbed out, after cutting off his useless dick of course. I only have to pick up the phone.

The normal cost of a young girl or boy for the night is twenty dollars, that's with their bottoms plugged – unplugged is negotiable. If you buy four or more at once, you can get a discount like in a supermarket. The terms of business are beat-up old words like: 'short time', 'long time', 'jiggy-jiggy', 'sucky-sucky' and of course 'massage'. But as a guidebook to the city is careful to point out, a Thai massage is no ordinary massage: 'A Thai massage is where the young lady uses *every* part of her body to massage *every* part of your body . . . Thai girls are well known for their smallness.'

The government bans the import of pornographic materials. Who in their right mind would export pornography to Bangkok? For a hundred dollars anyone can be their own porno-star for the night.

The first night, I sat in the hotel lobby and watched the tourists and businessmen bringing back their sexual trophies. I saw a fat businessman with three whores. The oldest was probably sixteen. They were gathered round him like tugs bringing an ocean liner to dock and he had an expression on his face that said, 'Look at me. See how virile and potent I am. I have three women here and I am going to take them upstairs and fuck the living daylights out of them.' He can make as much noise as he likes when he gets to his room and gets down to business as it is the proud boast of the hotel management that 'all our rooms are soundproofed, so the businessman will not be disturbed at critical moments'.

Looking at this fat businessman, I would imagine the only critical moment he will have in Bangkok is when he tries to attain and maintain a suitable erection. The whole 'business' thing in Bangkok is a farce. The only business done in this 'City of Angels' is sex. Every nationality is here: Japanese, English, American, German, and so on, thousands of them every night, all thrusting themselves into prime young Thai flesh. A butcher's shop full of flesh and dripping with sperm.

Business in the 'City of Angels' is done like this: 'Here is twenty dollars. Now lay down and open your legs and make loud groaning noises until I come.' This arrangement seems to satisfy everybody. It is the ultimate overkill of sexual pleasure. When you really can have everything you want, then you don't want it any more.

Outside the hotel is no better.

Everyone you meet in the street wants to know whether, 'You wanna fuck, Johnny?'

Or, 'You wanna blow-job, Johnny?'

They offer sex like other people offer cigarettes.

'You wanna see something special, Johnny?'

I just shook my head and kept on walking. The fiftieth man was more persuasive.

'Come on Johnny, I show you something very special.'

'Like what?' I asked him.

He came closer.

'Live sex show, Johnny. Very beautiful girls.'

'That's not special. I can watch people fucking anywhere, even in my own mirror,' I replied.

'Animals, Johnny. Girls and animals, I can show you.'

'What sort of animals?'

'Dogs, Johnny.'

I looked at him, he was smiling.

'I tell you what, *Johnny*,' I said. 'If you can show me a chicken fucking a rabbit I'll give you a hundred bucks.'

His smile disappeared, lickety-split. His eyes narrowed and went very hard.

'Don't fuck with me, Johnny!' he warned.

'Well, you are the first person who has said that to me in Bangkok, *Johnny*,' I told him.

I left him and found a small local bar and sat down. The man serving asked me, 'You wanna pretty girl? Very tight, very young.'

His hands described his words.

'Just a beer, thanks. But make sure it's very tight and very young.'

A Thai man came and sat down next to me. He seemed OK. He didn't make personal enquiries about my sex life or offer me anything hotter than a cold beer. We drank a few beers together and made conversation about Europe. He wanted to visit Europe.

Suddenly things went wrong.

Walls started to tilt and grow higher. Events and people slipped away into a haze which started to run like an old film clip, slow, so that you could see the frames in between, faces jumped back and forward. The beer bottle developed a bend in the middle and started transforming itself into a dirty drainpipe that got higher and higher until it jammed itself noisily into the ceiling. Cracks ran down the walls from the impact and the beads of water on the bottle that was now a drainpipe turned into a flood that slopped out of the door in little waves. A cigarette pulled itself out of the packet with tiny hands, grew small feet and walked across the table, climbed up my shirt and jumped into my mouth. A Zippo lighter with small wings floated in front of my eyes and lit my cigarette. When I inhaled, I looked down at my body and could see the smoke curling through my lungs. I reached for the beer glass and it grew tiny legs as well and scuttled across the table, then leaped off with a loud shriek. I watched it run across the road, spilling beer, and finally hide under a food stall. It looked like a very frightened little beer glass.

Some musical notes danced in the air and popped like balloons with a pleasant chime-like sound. Then someone came along with a big pot of black paint and a brush and started filling up all the available space. I tried to peer around the blackness, but he was painting too fast. It ended there. I knew what it was.

I'd been there before. Some bastard had finned me. Either that, or I was having a very bad flashback.

In Bermuda we used to shoot a tab of mescaline or acid every night, sometimes two. I had to give up after one year as I was into twenty-four-hour, heavy-duty flashbacks, and even a cigarette could push me into a bad trip that I didn't want or couldn't control and it was getting very dangerous. I nearly killed a guy, in the Princess Hotel disco in Hamilton harbour one night, with a heavy glass ashtray when I thought he was pointing a gun at me. He was actually lighting a cigarette and I only missed him by an inch. The guys hustled me out of there pretty damn quick. God . . . I just thought, I was sixteen then.

I laid off after that.

But I remember how it was.

Maybe this wasn't mescaline or acid but it was something close, or maybe I was finally going crazy. This was a strong possibility, as I've been borderline for many years. Just ask my friends. If you can find any of them.

I woke up the next day in a hotel room. Nothing strange in

that, except it was not my hotel room. My hotel room had carpets, wallpaper, mini-bar, telephone and all those other things they give you. This room had a full-length mirror, a television mounted on the wall, and nothing else apart from a lot of dirt and the bed I was dying in. My head felt like it'd been shot with something of a high calibre and my body felt like it had been torn apart by an angry musk-ox. Every muscle screamed at every movement. The television was on, casting an ugly blue glow around the room. It was the only source of light. There was no window. Images flickered across the screen. They resolved into what I expected them to be. People thrusting and grunting, shoving whatever they could manage into wherever they could manage it. I felt vacant. Drained. Ten minutes later I got the hell out of there.

A small Thai man blocked my path. He looked as dangerous as anybody I had ever seen in my life. He held his skinny hand out and rubbed his thumb and forefinger together.

'One thousand Bhat,' he said in a voice that slithered across the floor between us like a black cobra.

I reached in my pocket and found nothing. Last night I'd had about ten thousand Bhat in there.

'No money. All gone,' I told him.

His sympathy was palpable.

'Money,' he said softly, still rubbing his thumb and finger together, and now there were two snakes writhing on the floor with their hoods raised.

Another Thai guy appeared, from nowhere it seemed, and simply whacked a handful of notes into the man's hand, grabbed my shoulder and led me past him.

'You OK?' he asked when we were outside.

'No. I'm not OK,' I assured him.

'I'll see you to your hotel. This is a very dangerous area . . . Come on.'

'What about the money?' I asked.

'Tonight.'

I never saw him again. Perhaps he really did help me, or perhaps he was part of the whole thing. Whatever the 'whole thing' was.

I slept through most of the day. When I finally woke up I

realised that I had an irrational fear that would not go away. I couldn't even say to myself what it was. I was just scared to bloody death of everything. If I looked at anything for too long it began to move in that funny acid-induced way. Patterns of light scampered across the floor too quickly for me to really see and the slightest noise or movement made my whole body freeze. My brain was whirling and my body was hot. Sweat poured out of my hands. I hit the whisky bottle and my nerves flattened out. I started to pull out some sort of control over the brain. The spin came to an end but the machine was still running wild, the hands shook like dead leaves blowing in a breeze and the stomach was a butterfly farm full of freaked-out specimens. When the bottle was empty I went to the coffee-shop and tried to have a meal but ran out in absolute terror when the waiter asked me what I wanted. I had room service bring up something instead. I ate it, it tasted good. Then I walked into the toilet and – without even realising it – threw it all up in the sink. I tried to take a walk outside, but that was even worse. Everything and everybody was a threat. The same threat followed me back into the hotel room, it felt like someone had their hands round my throat all the time, I couldn't breathe, I was going to suffocate. I drank more whisky, I drank gin, I threw up again. That was enough.

I packed my bag, put extra-dark sunglasses on, and checked out. My bill was an amazing $1,000, all drink. I got a taxi to the airport. There was a Garuda International Jumbo Jet wedged into the arrivals hall. You could see its nose sticking through the smashed plate-glass window when you walked in. That's what day it was: the day a 747 arrived in the arrival hall of Bangkok International Airport. I think I punched someone, don't know who it was. I walked on the first flying machine I could find and got the hell out of there. On the flight some turkey started telling me about his sex holiday in Bangkok and it took three stewards to get my hands off his throat and strapped back into my seat. They wouldn't serve me any alcohol after that, bastards! My whole body shook like I was getting electric shock treatment for the entire flight, and in the end I had the tail section of the plane all to myself. And here I am in Singapore on the twenty-fourth storey of some monstrous hotel having a nervous breakdown.

I recognise the symptoms . . . withdrawal, cold turkey, plain ordinary madness, call it what you like. Maybe someone slipped me something very dangerous and I am now wanting more. Or perhaps I am really going crazy. I keep thinking I am.

But I've been here before. Been in Singapore before and had a black wall put up in front of my eyes and nearly gone crazy. It was a different Singapore then, not this sanitised, George Orwell version of Washington DC where everyone runs around with personal bleepers and people get caught pissing in elevators. The old Singapore has disappeared beneath a high-rise concrete wave of America. Kentucky Fried Chicken, MacDonalds, Pizza Hut, Barbie Dolls, American Express Gold Cards and 'Have a nice day y'all', courtesy of my old hand-shaking friend Mr Lee Kuan Facking Yew. I should have kicked him in the balls there and then at the school in 1967, maybe I could have prevented all this shit.

Sir Thomas Stamford Raffles is probably rotating in his grave at a speed of about five hundred miles per hour with the thought that his dream has turned into just another American outpost of Coca-Cola and Big Mac. In the official government tourist guidebook to Singapore, on page fourteen, is a picture of Raffles' statue, the caption underneath reads: *What would Raffles say if he could see Singapore today?*

I reckon what the good old boy would say is: 'Holy Shit! Who the hell are all these foreigners?'

2

I never did bother with Raffles Hotel. This was not snob-bery but the result of a very poor education in that I had never heard of: Noel Coward, Rudyard Kipling, Joseph Conrad, Somerset Maugham. In fact, at that time I had never even heard of Raffles or his hotel. I was brought up in a different world. I could catch fish as good as anyone in the kampong and could run along to a cock-fight with Richard Chan and bet my pocket-money on one of his birds and win enough to go out and get drunk with him for four days. If I had got into Raffles and someone had told me that Somerset Maugham wrote *The Moon and Sixpence* in his personal suite looking out over the Palm Court I would have ignored them and said, 'Get me an ice-cold Tiger beer, will you, there's a good chap.'

I left school when I was thirteen after making the simple decision that education was a waste of time when compared to the benefits of fishing or cock-fighting. My parents didn't notice for a long while. Mother always had her nose in a book and father was always away.

My serious drinking was done in the Union Jack Club, simply because that was one of the only places that would serve us kids with beer and let us put it on our father's tab – a deadly combination which resulted in my having to leave home for long periods and live in the kampong with cock-fighting friends like Richard Chan, eating goat-meat curries and playing mah-jong till the sun came up and then going fishing, while my father spat blood trying to figure out how he had spent $200 in the Union Jack Club in Singapore when he had just spent the last three months fighting communists in Borneo.

What also attracted me to the Union Jack Club was its clientele: rough, hard soldiers and sailors who didn't give a damn about anything and sat on the rusty metal chairs downing jugs of Tiger until they were so full that the stuff ran out of their armpits and made them stink like baboons on heat. Then they would go outside and throw up on a trishaw driver and eventually be thrown into the back of a taxi and whipped down to Boogey Street, where their mortal remains would be put on view for everyone's amusement until they got their act together again and found an attractive, tawny-brown girl who was prepared to ignore the smell and the vomit down the front of their shirt for a large fee. And nobody seemed to mind, when they got down to the serious business of copulation, that the tawny-brown girl turned out to be a man. 'What the hell, she looks like a million dollars, and is only costing me twenty! What the hell, nobody knows any different and I haven't had a piece of tail for two months, stuck on that stinking ship.'

That was Boogey Street in those days. Now it's all bull-dozed down and you have to call sex 'massage services'.

We used to spend a lot of time on Boogey Street, me and Carl. Carl was a friend who shared my views about educa-tion, fishing and cock-fighting for a while and we used to raise a lot of hell together. One night we had been in the Union Jack drinking Tiger on Carl's father's bill – it was his turn rather than my father's. We were always very fair about that.

Every time we downed a jug we would toast him, 'To Major Ryan. God bless him!' we would shout, standing up and raising our glasses. Then we'd fall over with laughing.

The waiters liked us and would make us special ham-burgers smothered in mango sauce and raw onions. Some-times they let us sleep on the floor, which was a lot better than sleeping on Jardine Steps – our normal place – waiting for the boat to arrive at six to take us back to my island.

One particular night we were well gone with drink and decided to look over the scene at Boogey Street. We never had any money but could usually score a few beers off some drunken servicemen who liked watching kids attacking Tiger beer like seasoned pros.

As we left the club we saw a Corporal score a direct hit on a trishaw man with a disgusting stream of vomit before being thrown into a taxi by his wobbly comrades.

'First class!' screamed Carl in hysterics. We took the poor guy's trishaw as a compensatory gesture. They took this sort of behaviour from us civilised people very well, and the guy was soon grinning at us and shouting out as we worked our way through the narrow streets, 'Hey boys! I get you very good girls. Jiggy-jiggy plenty good. Jiggy-jiggy, one fuck ten buck!'

You couldn't get a car into Boogey Street after seven at night because they closed the road down and ran food stalls all across it. Lights were strung up over the street and the whole place screamed out 'Party, party!' for ten hours every night. A person could get anything on Boogey Street. There were even opium dens just like in one of my old *Tintin* comics. And the best food in the world cooked right in front of you, like *hokkien mee*, thick yellow noodles swimming with prawns and squid and hot enough to get the grease off your tongue. One of our favourites was 'Buddha jumps over the wall'. We just liked ordering, 'Hey! Give us two Buddhas jumping over a wall!'

Roti John was what all the trishaw men ate, and we had a special stall for that. The guy who ran it had a big gold ring on his finger and would crack the eggs open about four foot above the wok with the ring. We could watch him for hours. He used to give us free Horlicks as well, never mind that it was boiled up in one of his old socks. Yes, the best food in the world. And while you ate it, the best whores in the world sauntered past exchanging obscene comments with the drunks who were trying to drink enough Tiger beer to get up the courage to take one of them upstairs and find out she was a man and still go through with it.

That night me and Carl were leaning against a wall watching the action, looking for an easy mark for a few beers.

Two classic looking whores walked past us and called out the usual stuff. We ignored them but they turned back to us anyway. One came right up to Carl and pinned him against the wall with her hips so he couldn't move.

'Hey, cherry-boy. Got five bucks in your pants?' she asked. She was extremely gorgeous and at least a foot taller than either of us. I'm convinced that if we had had five dollars we would have been upstairs in twenty seconds, never mind the pain in the penis the next day and pleading with the army doctor not to tell my father because he would just rip my head off and feed my remains to the kampong dogs and forget that he had ever conceived me in a moment of passion somewhere.

Her hair came down to her backside and she was as slim and willowy as anything. She started to undo Carl's zip and he started to look one hundred per cent frantic. Then suddenly she stepped back and in one fluid motion lifted her long batik skirt up around her waist.

Man! Oh, man!

She had a penis under there . . . Which made us realise we had a lot more growing to do before we could play at being big boys. She waved this brown projectile at us while a load of other whores fell about on the street laughing their heads off.

'You kids better go home to mother before I decide to play with you,' she warned us and we lit out, fast.

'Jesus! She was a man!' I said to Carl when we stopped for air at the other end of the street..

'Your grasp of sexual matters leaves me in awe,' Carl said. He was two years older than me.

'Imagine taking her to the next school dance,' I said, and Carl cracked up.

We looked the tables over at that end of the street. On one was a guy in a strange uniform, all by himself, knocking back Tiger beer like he thought Mr Lee Kuan Facking Yew might introduce prohibition at midnight. His eye caught mine and he looked us over. He stood up and waved to us. I looked at Carl and he gave me a discreet thumbs up.

The guy was a Yank. The first Yank I ever met in my life.

'You guys wannahaveabeerwithme?' it sounded like.

17

We said, 'Well, sure,' and sat down.

The guy ordered beers by the half-dozen and we were certainly into that – after making sure he knew that we didn't have two cents to rub together of any sort of dollar.

'Sheet!' he said. 'I got plenty of dollars. Drink up. What are two young guys like you doing in Boogey Street for Christ's sake? This is one dangerous place.'

'We can take care of ourselves,' Carl assured him, then knocked back a whole bottle of beer in case the Yank doubted it. I did the same. We both belched very loudly, making the Yank laugh. Every so often either Carl or me would stand up and make the usual toast.

'To Major Ryan. God bless him!'

This really cut the Yank up.

'Are you an American soldier?' I asked.

'Hell, no! I'm a Marine, boy. One of God's finest. Out for a bit of R and R on good old Boogey Street.'

'What's R and R?' Carl asked in a slurry voice. We were way over the top.

The Yank grinned. 'That's what I'm trying to find out, son.'

'You have to be careful on Boogey Street,' Carl told him.

'The hell I do!' he exclaimed.

We told him about the whore with the gigantic penis and warned him that even some of the best looking girls on the street turned out to be men in drag upon closer inspection. 'Sheet! I know what to do with one of them,' he told us, and we believed him.

He had short sleeves on his uniform and his muscles were like iron. He looked as hard as a hammer and was the type of guy you wanted around you on Boogey Street if things went wrong. We were feeling really confident with this Yank.

We chatted and drank beers for a long time and he seemed an OK guy so when he asked us whether we wanted to go to a nightclub – he was paying – we thought 'Why the hell not?'

It was a Chinese nightclub, full of whores, transvestites and gangsters somewhere round the back of the New World Stadium. I wouldn't have normally gone into a Chinese nightclub, it could cost you your life, but we were way out of

18

our heads by then. Richard Chan sometimes took me with him to the clubs after cock-fighting but with Richard a body was safe anywhere in Singapore.

We started into the black rice wine. I knew it was a bad mistake because that is one evil drink which can send you into either permanent blindness or madness or both. But we drank it, I guess because we were only thirteen and when you are thirteen you are pretty bloody stupid about everything. OK, so Carl was fifteen but the extra two years made no difference. Anyway, that was it. Everything turned into a white wall, then a black wall, then nothing but some obscure movement, a few bright lights and then the black wall again.

' . . . great whirling pits, round and round they go. Lay still and they go away. Lay still, not round and round, whirling, whirling . . . Oh shit! You moved, you idiot! Now you have to be sick, now you have to get to the bog without waking Father up. Oh shit! Last time you were sick in the hallway and he killed you . . . I'm going to be sick.'

I woke up in a strange room in a strange bed and I had no clothes on. The room was bright but my eyes wouldn't focus straight. I leaned over the side of the bed and threw up on the floor.

Finally my eyes focused on a door. It opened and the Marine came in, stark naked, pulling Carl, who was also naked, behind him by the hand.

Someone had hit the Marine with a transformer ray or something. He had undergone a *radical* change, as if someone had wiped his face with an acid cloth to reveal another underneath. This new face was warped and crooked, like the painted mask of a circus clown on a heavy lysergic trip. He had put make-up on his eyes and his lips were a violent, ugly red that made a split across his face the colour of fresh blood. He clapped his hands together at the sight of me, released Carl, bent his thick, hairy knees in a girlish manner and screamed in a high falsetto, 'Oh! My lovely little girl has woken up. How is her little head?'

He crept over the carpet towards me and I sobered up at over one thousand miles an hour. You could hear the sonic boom as my brain went to all stations red. Carl just stood vacantly in the doorway. I thought it was the end of my life. Just before he reached the bed, a door behind me which I hadn't seen was ripped suddenly off its hinges and thrown with a loud crash into the room. The Marine hit the brakes. A whole load of men poured into the room. I was confused as hell. The Marine made a dive for the bathroom but they grabbed him, and Carl. They were all big men with hard crewcuts.

Two muscular black guys held the Marine by the throat and shoulders against the wall. His feet dangled a foot off the floor. The other four men were white. They all looked at me with madness in their eyes. Two of them were holding naked Carl, slumped between them. One of the big black guys pulled back his fist and smashed the Marine as hard as he could, right in the mouth. There was a sickening crunch of teeth breaking and blood flew across the room, spattering the bed and me and spraying the wall behind the men. The Marine slid down the wall like a wet rag. One of the white guys shouted, 'Frigging queers! A whole room full of frigging queers!' Then they threw Carl back into the bathroom and started to kick and pummel him. He was squealing like a schoolgirl. I could hear the men shouting in the bathroom.

'Frigging little fairy!'

'Piss on him!'

'Stick his queer little head down the john and piss on him!'

I guess that is what they did. Then they came out for me. I looked around for my clothes but couldn't see them, so pulled the sheet around me. I think I was praying for the very first time in my life.

'Oh dear God. Help me for Christ's sake!' I was saying to myself, over and over again.

Four of them stood around the bed and stared at me, absolutely berserk. The Marine was doubled up on the floor, sobbing and spitting out blood. The two black guys came out of the bathroom with Carl and dragged him over to the big French windows.

'Watch this you little frigging queer,' one of them said to me.

Two of the white guys grabbed me and hauled me over to the window. Carl was delirious. Blood was sluicing from his nose and mouth. They opened the window and picked Carl up by the hands and feet and started to swing him backwards and forwards. I said, 'You can't . . . ' But one of the white guys smashed me in the mouth and I couldn't speak for blood. On the count of ten, with a big whoop of joy, they threw Carl straight out of the window. The room was on the third floor.

I don't know whether these guys knew it or not but there was a swimming pool in the courtyard below and Carl sailed into that with a splash. He lived.

I was still in the room with these one hundred per cent lunatics.

'See! Fairies can fly,' one of the white guys told me. They all found that really funny and maybe it was, but not to me, not at that particular moment in time. It was very bloody unfunny.

They pulled me back to the bed and threw me on it. The Marine had done a runner while we were all at the window. I didn't blame him. These guys were probably on leave from Vietnam and obviously capable of murder and more. They were also totally out of their brains on God knows what.

'We ought to kill you, little fairy,' the same white guy who had punched me in the mouth told me in a cold, dead voice.

'I'm only thirteen for Christ's sake, and I'm not a fairy,' I said, with blood running down my chin and dripping onto the bed. The truth was that I didn't have one single idea what the hell a frigging fairy was – unless they meant little creatures dressed in tutus with wings and magic wands, and I don't believe they did.

Jesus! He really went into overdrive at that and just attacked me, slapping me around the head and punching my ribs.

'BASTARD! WRITING ON WALLS, YANKEE GO HOME . . . LITTLE FRIGGING FAIRY . . . COMMUNIST FRIGGING COCK-SUCKING FRIGGING HIPPY FRIGGING QUEER PERVERT DIRTY LITTLE ARSE-LICKING COMMIE LONG-HAIRED FRIGGING QUEER!'

21

It went on and on until one of the black guys stopped him and they had a conference in whispers. Then they had a good laugh. The biggest guy started to unbuckle his trousers. The others watched, grinning.

One of them then put his mouth close to my ear and said, 'Oh, pretty boy, you are going to get fucked. You are going to get so fucked that you ain't never gonna forget it. That's what you came here for, isn't it, pretty boy?'

I prayed for anything. Jesus! This was not happening. This was only in my mind. These guys were going to hurt me very bad and I had done nothing – except get drunk. I wished Richard Chan could walk in the room right then. He would have torn those guys apart and you needn't have looked for the pieces. I once saw a guy stick a knife in his throat outside a cock-fight one night and Richard just tensed his neck muscles and all he had was a nick in the skin. Then he exploded into white lightning that rippled and crackled until the man with the knife was floating through the rusty metal side of the cinema like it was made of paper. He was dead before he hit the floor. But Richard was not going to walk through the doorway. Why not? Jesus! Richard! Walk through that door. Now! Now!

One of the other guys had found my trousers and was going through the pockets. He took a small card out and looked at it. It was my ID.

His face changed.

'Jesus!' he said. 'This guy's father is a fucking captain in the British fucking army.'

Nobody moved. It was as if someone had stopped this surreal film in mid-frame, one guy with his trousers round his ankles and the others frozen where they stood.

I got up off the bed very carefully, walked across the room, took my trousers off the man holding them, put them on – couldn't see my shirt and I never wore shoes anyway – then I walked out of the room, very slowly. They still did not move, they were still looking at the ID as if it might bite them. I hadn't taken one single breath the whole time. I reached the stairs and said into my Mickey Mouse wristwatch, 'Beam me up, Spock. Let's get the hell out of here!'

Then I went down those stairs f-a-s bloody t.

I never saw Carl again after that night. I know *why* I didn't see Carl after that. He didn't want to see me any more. When Carl walked through the door with that crazy Marine as I was just coming round, the bastard was smiling . . . He was enjoying himself, until those guys arrived and messed things up for him.

3

Christ, it's hard to imagine all that now, sat in this shitty little hotel room in Singapore, lodged somewhere between a very unfriendly now, a decidedly sticky future and a past that got me into nothing but a load of bloody trouble. I've got the television on. I always have the television on, twenty-four hours a day, even if it's only a buzzing noise. I have to kill the silence . . . I can't take that silence. It trips me out, very quickly. I'd rather not have the television on, because I keep seeing things which remind me of the Boss and that's the last thing I want to be reminded of. But you can't get away from that slippery fat toad. Or maybe it's me I can't get away from. I just thought of that. If I'm running away from myself then I am in deep trouble.

There is an advert from Mr Lee Kuan Facking Yew's raving family-planning maniacs who, after controlling the population of Singapore almost to extinction, have finally realised their stupid mistake and are now producing slushy spots with the theme 'The best thing you can give your child is a sister or a brother.' Abortions are now out, folks. Get down to a bit of honest copulation . . . Mr Lee wants a bigger army, sorry, 'People's Defence Force'.

Abortions! Christ! The word takes me back.

Did you ever lose track of normality? What's right and what's wrong? You wake up and find yourself still drunk on a 747 sitting in first class and escorting a couple of giggling tarts to Harley Street for an expensive abortion – a couple of the Boss's many mistakes – and you carrying on drinking the champagne because you can't think of anything better to do. Then suddenly, and with no warning whatsoever, comes this moment of brilliance in the heavy clouds of champagne, a point of absolute clarity, and you shake your head and say to yourself: 'This is not normal . . . No, this is very fucking un-normal!'

So you ask one of the giggling tarts, 'Is this normal?'

She reflects long enough to throw a glass of Moet et Chandon down her throat, then replies. 'Listen, darling, I'm getting seventy-five thousand bucks for this little trip. So don't be a lollipop, be a dear and order another bottle of this French anti-freeze.'

There's no point in asking the other one about normality, she's not been allowed to open her mouth for the last four years, except for practical reasons. She looks like a million dollars but when she opens her mouth it's an icy blast from Putney.

How did I ever get wrapped up in this sort of shit anyway? I just wanted to stay on my island with someone reliable, like Richard Chan, and I end up being plastered all over the world in the company of lunatics, slave-traders and homicidal maniacs. I mean, who gets themselves almost beat to death in the harbour of St Lucia, Virgin Islands? Other people go there for a holiday. Who in the hell gets stabbed in the back in a New York bar when they're only sixteen? And who ends up being employed by a rabid toad like the Boss?

Jesus! I was complaining about whores and exploitation earlier on, when to all intents and purposes I have been nothing better than a pimp for the last three years of my life. Is that all it is? Just plain ordinary guilt combined with a lifelong madness that's driven me to the point where I may just throw myself out of that window? Is my nervous breakdown really me feeling sorry for myself, sorry and guilty? Am I going to do what I always do – get to the top then throw it all away again? I've got a house in England in a lovely village, complete with wife and dog and stacks of money in the bank . . . But I don't want any of it. You can take that Mercedes

560 coupé sat outside my front door and you can stuff it anywhere you like. Stuff everything . . . I couldn't care less.

No matter what I do, no matter where I go, it never matches the past: old Singapore, the island, Richard Chan, my dogs. Maybe it never will.

Once I had the hotel a long way behind me I stopped running and walked. I was talking to myself and swearing out loud. Some Chinese women stopped and looked at me.

'How the hell did Carl get away with no clothes on?' I asked them.

They ran off, frightened, with tiny little steps.

Click, click, click.

Click. A policeman, a great big Sikh, stopped as well and I could feel his eyes on my back as I walked away. He didn't stop me – probably came to the conclusion that I was one of the White Russians who lived in absolute poverty in the backstreets of Singapore in those days. I once saw one stood outside a dirty eating house, begging, and he was stark naked. I was so moved that I gave him my last fifty cents and told him to buy some pyjama bottoms, but he didn't understand me.

I walked and walked. I think I was in shock or something. Finally I got to Orchard Road and there was our favourite roadside stall by the old cold storage building. I sat down and asked the old guy for a Horlicks, even though I didn't have any money. I drank my Horlicks and made three wishes:

First wish: that Carl gets run over by a Changi bus.

Second wish: that the Yanks would get their arses well and truly kicked by Mr Ho Chi Canting Min. (Thank you God for granting that one.)

Third wish: that someone would give me some money to pay for the Horlicks.

Some late-night tourists arrived and sat opposite me. They were looking at me and whispering. I suppose I looked pretty bloody dreadful, all beaten up and half naked. A smooth looking woman, she was probably a three-hundred-dollar whore, got up and came over to me.

'You poor thing . . . Here, take this, please,' she said, and held out a ten dollar note. I don't think my hand ever moved so fast. She jumped back.

'You haven't got twenty cents as well, have you, please,' I asked in my best English schoolboy accent.

She fiddled in her purse.

'Why do you need the twenty cents?' she asked as she handed the coins over to me.

'Well, I'm going down to Boogey Street and buying a whore with the ten dollars. I need the twenty cents to pay for the Horlicks.'

She stomped back to her friends.

I sat and thought about revenge on the Yanks. This is what would happen: Me and Richard would be waiting outside their hotel. When they came out, laughing and looking forward to a night on the town whoring and drinking, Richard would glide over and cream them. No fuss about it, he would just hit them so hard that they would have to take their shoes off to crap . . . But it was no use. I was too tired and beat up even for revenge. I used the lady's money not for a Boogey Street whore but for a cab home, home to my island.

I reckon most parents would have had a fatal cardiac seizure if their son had come home in the condition I did. After being wasted by those Yanks in the privacy of a hotel room, I was bruised bad – swollen eyes, swollen lips, swollen ribs – but they didn't notice. They had given up noticing, or trying to curb my impulses to associate with gangsters and wander the bad backstreets of Singapore. I didn't blame them. You can only bash a child's head so many times against a concrete wall.

My older brother, Dave, did notice, God bless his gold tooth and black heart. He sat up in bed – we shared a room – and rubbed his eyes. It was eight in the morning.

'Have you been arguing with trains again?' he asked.

I threw myself down on the bed, the dogs jumped up with me. Punching the dogs gently I asked them, 'Why couldn't you pair of rabid, vicious bastards have been there, eh?'

'Well?' he asked.

'I don't want to talk about it,' I said.

'Bad?' he asked.

'Very bad.'

'Tell me about it then.'

'I don't want to talk about it!'

'Why not?'

'If I talk about it, I'll cry and you know I never cry.'

'Oh no, you're just too bloody tough to cry, aren't you? Jesus! Your face looks bloody awful. Who the hell did that to you?'

'The United States bloody cavalry, OK?' I said. He gave up then.

Ten minutes later I asked him, 'Do you know what a fairy is?'

'Peter Pan was a fairy,' he replied.

'Oh,' I said, and fell asleep.

This was a real period of disasters for me, and my brother, and the whole family come to that. The first disaster came a few days after my beating and almost deflowering by the Yanks. The school, outraged by my continued absence, sent a strong letter to my parents and they handcuffed me and delivered me to the school.

I hated it. I never hated anything more than to sit in one of those dreary classrooms with some idiot telling me about Cromwell or how to dissect a frog, when I could have been crouching in the dust of a cock-fight or spear-fishing with Richard Chan. And the kids gave me a very bad time, because I was not normal. I refused to wear the school uniform, went about on bare feet and had hair hanging down to my shoulders. Worse, much worse than all the rest, my friends were Chinese and Malay.

One guy in particular was gunning for me in an evil way. He was the school hard man, a sixth-former who had a pathological hatred of me and did anything and everything he could to make my life hell. I used to hide in the bogs for most of the day. One time he came in and stood combing his wavy blond hair. I was sat on a sink smoking a bidi.

'Every time I come in this bog I see you, filth,' he told me, looking at me in the mirror. 'You are a bog-rat, a Chogee bog-rat.'

Chogee was what guys like him called the locals. To call a nice white boy a Chogee was a mortal insult, but I was quite proud to be called a Chogee. A stiff shit like him would never have understood that. I ignored him and watched the smoke spiralling up from my bidi. I was scared of him but wasn't going to let him know that.

'Well, filth?' he demanded.

'Well what?' I asked.

'Well, are you a Chogee bog-rat or not, filth?'

'If you say so.'

He came up to me and shoved me hard up against a mirror and stuck his face right up in front of mine. His breath was fresh and minty. In fact he was so perfect he should have been in an underpants advert.

'Yeah!' he breathed. 'Yeah, I say so and I also say the next time I see you outside this school I'm going to beat the shit out of you. You are scum, filth, a disgrace to everybody, running around with Chinks and Chogs, dressed like a bloody wog!'

He threw me hard onto the floor and strode out, shaking his head. If the school hard man says you are a Chogee bog-rat, then the rest of the kids agree, and everywhere I went I got a bad time. They knocked my food out of my hands, spat in my milk bottle and trod on my bare feet. After one week I'd had enough and was contemplating running away – God knows where to, but just out of there, away.

Later I found myself stood at the side of the swimming pool for our after-school diving lesson. I spotted an unloaded spear gun with a shaft lying by it. Our instructor was in the water putting a kid through the passing-the-mouthpiece act. The school hard man arrived with some of his good old boys and they all leaned against the changing-room wall and looked at me with the simple threat of beating the shit out of me as soon as school was out. That was it. I picked up the spear gun, loaded the shaft, and sprung the weapon. It felt very good in the hand.

'Hey, dipstick!' I called out. The hard man pushed himself off the wall and looked at me.

'Yeah, you, dipstick,' I said and lifted the gun until it was centred on his perfect head. He went white white white and his friends found a time warp and walked into it. They were gone, he was frozen. I shifted my aim a tiny fraction and depressed the trigger. There was a loud whoosh and the shaft smacked into the wood panelling about a foot away from his head with a very satisfying thud. He was a shaking, gibbering mess on the floor. I walked over to him and kicked him up the arse.

'Did you shit yourself, filth?' I asked, and dropped the gun on him.

I took myself over to the Headmaster's room and sat down outside. He came out.

'What do you want?' he demanded.

'I think you may want to expel me in a minute,' I answered.

He went back into his room shaking his head. The diving instructor arrived at a million miles an hour and my feet didn't touch the ground again until they had me outside the school gates. Expelled for life. Great!

I had no more trouble with the underpants advert.

There were some things I learned very early on from Richard Chan. Don't get me wrong, it wasn't anything like 'Grasshopper, the meaning of life is . . . ' or any of that sort of shit. Richard taught you stuff by just being Richard. You watched and you learned and one of the first things I learned was that you *do* let people push you around and mess you about. It doesn't cost anything. I'd seen guys be cheeky to Richard in nightclubs and him just sit there and take it, when I knew if he had wanted to he could have ended the rest of their lives in three seconds flat. But just let *anybody* touch him in the wrong place, like to do with his fighting cocks, family, friends or mah-jong game and you could can them up right away for dog meat. There is a limit, you let people come right up to that limit, but if they pass it, then you kill them.

One night, not long after I'd been expelled from school for attempted murder – that's what they called it – we had real big trouble and if there hadn't been a certain person called Richard Chan around this other certain person would not be drawing breath any more.

As usual the parents were not there: father was fighting the good fight and for all I know mother was in some kind of home trying to recover from her malevolent brood of sons. She wasn't there, I know that much, and I was sat reading Edgar and drinking Tiger. Then the amah started wailing and shrieking like Ho Chi Canting Min himself had just walked in the door or something. Reluctantly, I walked out onto the balcony to see the nature of our latest disaster.

Brothers! Did you ever have brothers? Jesus! They are more trouble than they are worth. There was my brother lying in a pool of blood and the amah on her knees in front of him pulling out her hair and shrieking fit to burst. I'll say this for my brother, he gave me a grin under the most difficult circumstances imaginable. His right cheek was cut wide-open from his eye to his mouth and when he grinned you could see his teeth through the hole in his face.

'You are a real dramatic,' I told him.

'Yeah, I know,' he said, still grinning.

'What the hell happened to you!'

He shrugged his shoulders. 'Two guys got me in the kampong. One held my arms, the other stuck a knife in my face.'

'Do you know the guys?'

'Sure I know them. Real bad boys. Nothing you can do.'

'The hell there isn't. I'll go and get Richard!'

'No you won't. Don't get Richard involved in this type of shit. It's my own fault. I was cheeky.'

'Well the least I can do is to get your sad carcass to a hospital,' I told him.

He shook his head. 'The whole kampong is in the middle of a mammoth riot. No way can you get down there and find us a Landrover or boat.'

'So what am I supposed to do?' I demanded, 'sit around and watch you bleed to death? I'd get the blame for it!'

The amah had reduced herself to the blubbering jelly level so I sent her back to her room. Dave picked himself up and wandered into the kitchen, leaving a trail of blood behind him. He opened the fridge, got a can of Tiger, cracked it and poured it into his mouth. Most of it ran out of the hole in the side of his face. I went and got my big Japanese sword, the one my father had picked up from somewhere and foolishly given me years ago, slung it over my back and whistled the two dogs up.

'Where are you going?' Dave asked.

'I'm going to get us a Landrover and a boat. You have got to get to a hospital.'

He cracked another can of beer. 'Good luck,' he said.

I started at a fast jog down the narrow road towards the kampong with the dogs at my heels. At least they were keen on this expedition.

Generally it was a bad time. Things had been building up for a long while. Our friend Mr Lee Kuan Facking Yew had been whipping up anti-British sentiment in an effort to cover up his own stupid political cock-ups and only a week before had given the British armed forces twenty-four hours to get the hell out of the country. He'd quickly withdrawn that when he realised that the Indonesian communists were just waiting to roll on his new republic and squash it flat into the ground like a dead beetle. Then a crazy Welsh corporal had let all the pigs out of the army slaughter yard on the island and driven them through the Malay part of the kampong. Some of them even ended up in the mosque and the Muslims were bloody angry about that. And it was coming on for Chinese New Year, always a good excuse for a few harmless riots. Living on a small island cut off from the mainland, trouble like this affected us a lot more than the people living on Singapore.

The kampong was a mess – people milling about all over

the place, stalls overturned, and a few small fires burning by the side of the road. Without looking left or right I walked straight down the centre of the road. A few people stopped and stared but nobody did anything. I thought I was home and running, but then a group of guys came out of the old metal cinema and ranged themselves across the road in front of me. It was just like in the bloody movies and I started whistling the theme from *For A Few Dollars More* or some such crap. I would have liked to laugh but these guys were carrying homemade baseball bats and one of the bastards had a metal stake or something and their expressions were about as friendly as my father's when discovering his dear children have drunk his last can of Tiger beer. I knew the guys all right, same ones that had stuck my brother – very bad news people. I stopped. They stopped. The dogs growled low in their throats and the guys shifted nervously. They knew my dogs. Then suddenly the biggest guy ran forward and tried to kick one of the dogs. His kick was wild and the dog got his fangs into his knee and was hanging on for death. The other dog got his arm and then all the guys started laying in with their clubs. One blow took all the air out of a dog and laid him flat on the ground. I whistled and one dog ran back to me, the other crawled. I put a hand over my back and fingered the handle of the sword. I was sweating like hell. If I pulled that sword, there was no going back. Someone was going to end up cut to pieces on the kampong dirt and I reckoned it would be me, dogs or no dogs. They had already stuck a knife in my brother's face and from there on in it was a very small step to beating me to death, a very small step indeed.

'Come on,' I pleaded. 'I only want to get to the jetty and get a boat. My brother is sick.'

One slimy looking guy called out, 'We know your brother is sick. All you bastards should be dead.'

You could tell from his pinched, weasel face that he was the one with the knife. They are always twisted little bastards and I couldn't help myself. I set the dogs on him. They were good like that, you could single out one thing with your hand and just say to them, 'You go and rip that to shreds' and they would.

It was a real mess for a while, with the dogs ripping his legs to bits and the guys trying to wallop them with the clubs. They managed to knock the air out of the injured one again, so I called them back. Both dogs ranged themselves round my legs, panting like hell and growling like dynamos gone out of control. We stood like that for a couple of minutes – a stand-off. Then the guys decided to call my bluff with the sword and the dogs. They moved forwards and I moved slowly back, keeping the dogs in front of me. In the deepest corner of my vision, not quite behind me, someone stepped out of the darkness and stood immobile by the side of the road. *Shit!* I thought and whirled quickly round, expecting a knife in the back or something.

It was Richard Chan.

He stood with a slight smile on his face. He had the usual ragged trousers on and no shirt. His arms were folded across his chest. He just stood there with that funny smile on his face. The guys stopped and looked at him. Nervous.

'Hey, Richard. We got no trouble with you,' the big guy said.

'Not yet you don't,' Richard said. The way he said it was so factual that it couldn't be denied. Those four simple words conveyed a blast of cold violence.

Then he moved. When Richard moved, you knew you were looking at something very special. You were looking at a predator. He pointed one arm in my direction, the muscles bunched so that nobody could mistake the power that lay just below the surface.

'He is a friend of mine,' he announced simply.

'He is English filth!' the big guy shouted, and spat on the road in his fury.

'Maybe he is, but he's still a friend of mine,' Richard replied, dead calm.

The big guy went to say something else, but before the rubbish spilled out of his head, Richard moved. He moved over the top of his own head, did three somersaults, blur-ringly fast, and landed on the point of his toes right in front of the guy's nose. He stayed there for about a millisecond, then went back over his own head so fast that his body made whipping noises as it tore through the air. He landed back where he had started from.

It was over.

It was a well-known fact all over Singapore, even amongst the Triads and other bad boys, that you did not cross Richard Chan and come out with a fortune cookie in your hand and a smile on your face. The men melted into the night. I let my breath out in one long sigh. I don't think I'd taken any air for the last minute and a half.

Richard stared at me with amusement.

'What would you have done if I hadn't been here? I could have been on the mainland with the birds.'

He meant the fighting cocks.

I shook my head. 'I don't know.'

He bent down and patted the dogs on the head. They knew him well enough.

'If you had just walked down here, without your dogs and without that sword, those guys would have left you alone. You know that, don't you? You challenged them.' He looked up at me.

'They knifed my brother,' I said.

'Your brother was cheeky. Come on, let's get you to the guardhouse and then your cheeky brother to the hospital. You can throw that sword in the sea.'

He took me to the guardhouse where the soldiers (they were local recruits and didn't want to get involved in any riots) had locked themselves in their cells for protection. We eventually persuaded them to come out with some rifles, and we took the caged Landrover and picked Dave up. There were no boats but a police launch went by and we hailed it over. They radioed ahead for an ambulance and it was waiting for us on Jardine Steps. I had to tell the cops that my brother had fallen down the stairs and cut his face on a sharp stone. We got him to the British Medical Hospital and they froze that side of his face. The doctor in casualty said if they used stitches he would be scarred for life. I reckon we all got scarred that night.

4

The behaviour of my brother Dave led me to strongly suspect that he was trying to outdo me. After I got beaten half to death, he had to go out and get himself knifed. Then he came up with an act that was bloody hard to follow: he got himself murdered.

Tragic, of course. My father could have killed him for it.

Dave had been away from home for a few days, at a massive party at Seletar Airbase or somewhere, so nobody was anxious about him. My parents didn't worry when we went missing for a week or so, they just breathed a huge sigh of contented relief. For a change my father was home, so I was on my best behaviour. Most of the time father was away fighting the communists down in Brunei or Borneo in the silly little war that they called the 'Confrontation'. He would be away for three months, then come home for a few days, go on an absolute bender, and then disappear again. For some reason whenever he was home he would take over the bathroom and sleep in there, so we all had to go dirty until he left again.

We were all living in a state of borderline madness in those days. Communists would land on the island late at night and blow our tiny power station to hell and back, always in the middle of a really rivetting episode of *The Invisible Man* or *The Lone Ranger*. This really upset the smaller brothers, who would be sat absolutely absorbed in the show, nursing their illegal cans of Tiger beer. Mother was always too interested in her book to notice the cans. When the lights suddenly went out she would shuffle about until she had found candles and then carry on reading as if nothing had happened.

Sometimes we could hear gun-fire during the night and one day I went down to the beach for my usual morning swim and there was a wrecked boat and dead bodies strewn all over the place. The commies had blown themselves away in a colossal explosion. I rushed into the breakfast room, excited and out of breath, waving a blackened, broken rifle.

'Mother!' I shouted. 'It's great! There's a load of dead bodies on the beach, all blown to hell! Blood all over the place . . . There's a leg in my canoe!'

'Do tell the amah what you want for breakfast, dear, she's waiting,' she said and carried on reading.

Very often we had armed guards around the house, day and night, and were forbidden to leave. Mother used to have terrible nightmares and come bursting into our rooms at three o'clock in the morning screaming, 'You are all dead! I saw you, covered in blood!' Or, 'They cut your heads off . . . I looked for them everywhere but I couldn't find them!'

This type of behaviour really relaxed us.

When father was at home he used to tote a machine gun and we did everything we could to persuade him to leave it with us when he went away to do his three months. He knew better.

Singapore early mornings were good. There was something about the sunlight stripping through the trees that caught you and kept you in bed in a state of suspended animation until lunchtime. I never got up until it was time for my morning swim, just before lunch. Unless I was fishing. Then I was out day and night for a week with Richard and the boys from the kampong.

I was enjoying just such a lazy, hazy Singapore morning in my bed on the day that my brother decided to get himself murdered. One dog was under the bed, the other brute was lying at the end of the bed on my feet, and the cat was curled up on the pillow by my head. This was to protect me from the large and voracious rats that lived in our house and garden and sometimes attacked us in the middle of the night. This worked most of the time, but only a couple of weeks before one rat had penetrated my elaborate bodyguard and bitten me on the throat. I killed that rat stone dead by smashing it against a wall in sheer panic. The dogs ripped it in half, then the cat ran away with the head. The bodyguard got a severe warning and a cut in rations for a week after that fiasco.

That morning the peace was shattered by a series of the most unearthly screams I had ever heard. They echoed around the house, moving from room to room, then entered the garden and proceeded to diminish down the small road that ran down the hill to the kampong.

'Shit!' I said to myself. I sat up in bed and looked out of the open window just in time to see the raving, maniacal form of my mother in her nightdress – clutching her hair and screaming for all she was worth – disappearing down the hill.

'Holy shit!' I shouted out aloud.

I already knew what to do in circumstances like this: put the dogs on red alert so that anyone entering the room would be torn to pieces, and then stick my head under the pillow and pray that I wasn't about to get involved in any bad news.

My father knew better than to just barge into my room unannounced: the dogs did not know him very well and might have gone for him. He hammered on the door while the dogs went berserk, ripping chunks of wood out of the frame and baying like bloodhounds.

'Call those ruddy animals off!' he roared.

I did and they sat on the bed, panting and glowering at the door.

Father poked his head around the door.

'Get dressed and go and get your mother. She's raving.'

'Jesus! Can't someone else go and get her?' I pleaded. This was very embarrassing.

I thought father was about to start frothing at the mouth.

'There is nobody here except you. GO AND GET YOUR BLOODY MOTHER!'

He rushed off to get his uniform on. We obviously had a very serious situation here. I threw my pants on and took off after mother at a fast run. I left the dogs locked in the bedroom – they would have really freaked out if they had seen mother fleeing in her nightgown and might have caused her serious damage.

Man! She was flying down that road, nightdress flowing behind her, screaming like a stuck pig. What a nightmare! She was about two hundred yards from the kampong and I had to stop her. As I was running after her I was thinking to myself, 'Somebody should be filming this shit.'

I brought her down with a strong tackle and managed to knock all the air out of her, which made her stop that awful screaming. She lay on the grass with lunacy in her eyes and kept saying, 'Dave! Dave! Dave!'

'Mother!' I told her. 'You have to come home. You are in your nightdress.'

It was like talking to a bar of soap. Her eyes rolled around in her head and she just kept saying 'Dave!' over and over again. I thought she couldn't stand the sight of any of us. Perhaps she had a lover called Dave, and father had just found out about it?

I threw her over my shoulder – mother was small – and started up the hill. Coming down the hill was father, in full uniform. He always looked damned good in uniform. Only dogs didn't like him in uniform, and always attacked him. As we passed each other he ordered, 'Go home and sit on her. Don't let her out of your sight.'

'What the hell is going on here?' I demanded.

He stopped and looked me full in the eyes, 'They just fished your brother's body out of the harbour, covered in stab wounds. Your brother has been murdered.'

'Oh sweet Jesus!' I said and started to shiver.

He marched off down the road and I took mother home.

Talk about bad. There was a Malay cop sat in the front room shifting his hat from hand to hand and looking as nervous as hell. He had obviously brought the news and my mother cracking up must have really upset him. Mother was delirious, so I locked her in her room. I put a couple of good belts of whisky into me and sorted the smaller brothers out – gave them a dozen cans of Tiger, sent them to their rooms and told them to shut up.

It was a harrowing morning. I spent the whole time thinking about the wicked things I had done to my brother in the past, like scratching his Bob Dylan records, and felt as bad as can be. The minutes went by like hours. The cop sat there. Nobody said anything. Then at one o'clock a full-blown hurricane came blasting into the room. It was my father. His face was redder than blood and I had never seen him look so crazy.

'YOU STUPID BASTARD!' he roared and attacked the policeman.

This was really getting out of hand. I sprang over and managed to pull him off the poor cop, only for a second, but it was long enough. The cop was gone, his feet skidding on the marble as he shot out of the room like a startled rabbit. Then father threw me off and was after him. They disappeared down the hill, but the cop looked to have the edge in speed. So would I with my father hot on my tail.

Five minutes later father was back. He got the whisky bottle and took a good gulp, then sat shaking his head and cursing softly under his breath. He always cursed in Chinese, and was very fluent at it.

'What is going on?' I asked him. I had first gear engaged and was riding the clutch just in case he had really gone stark raving mad.

He looked me over.

'That stupid policeman got the radio reports mixed up because his English is not very good. Your brother is not dead, though when I get hold of him he is going to wish he was.'

'Whose body was it then, and where exactly is Dave?' I asked.

'Your brother is in Changi prison on a charge of treason, for which the punishment is death, of course.'

'Holy smoke!' I said in admiration. I didn't know Dave had

that sort of stuff in him. This was going to give him real
celebrity status on the island, and all over Singapore.

'What he did was to pull the Singapore flag down off its
post in front of City Hall and burn it. I don't know who the
body belongs to, some Triad member or other I expect. No
doubt a friend of yours.'

The doctor arrived from the mainland and sedated
mother. She was a real mess for a long time after that. Just
behind the doctor was a CID Inspector from the Singapore
Police. I was sent out of the room while they negotiated. I
listened at the open window.

The Inspector said that they were not taking a serious view
of the case and would not press charges as they thought it was
a combination of youthful exuberance and too much Tiger
beer. He offered to have Dave released that day, but my
father told him, no, keep him locked up for a few days and
make the bastard sweat. The Inspector liked that and went
off happy.

My father lit out fast to go and fight commies in the south.
I guess he considered it easier work than dealing with the one
hundred per cent lunatics that made up his family.

Dave did become a celebrity, and everybody started calling
him Lazarus. But he had to avoid father for a very long time.
His first words to me when he came up over the hill and
walked into the house were, 'I suppose you sold all my Bob
Dylan records as soon as you heard I had kicked the bucket.'
I said to him, 'Just what are you going to do next, you
outrageous bugger?!'

What he did next was to sit on a branch of our massive
breadfruit tree and cut through it with a machete, so that
when it fell down he was still sat on it. I was in the shower and
heard the crash as the branch thudded into the garden from
twenty feet up. I also heard a long drawn out scream and then
sobbing. I didn't know anybody was cutting trees down and
assumed we had just taken a direct hit from an Indonesian

mortar. Then the amah started to wail and shriek – always a bad sign.

'I am not going out there to see what has happened,' I said to myself and turned the shower on full blast to drown out the sound of the sobbing and wailing. The amah started to beat on the door. As usual father and mother were away, this time in the Malaysian highlands, trying to recover some of their sanity after three years on a small island with us.

Confronted by the gibbering amah, I went outside expecting the worst, and that is exactly what I found. I couldn't believe it. This guy in front of me had scored the highest marks ever achieved in GCE A Level Pure Mathematics, Applied Mathematics, Technical Drawing, Physics, you name it. He was a genius.

He was a barely conscious genius.

The branch had fallen on top of him. It was a monster and had him pinned firmly to the ground. If the ground had been any harder he would have been dead. As it was, his arm and shoulder were smashed to pieces. I could see a bone sticking at least two inches out of his body from his shoulder joint and another jutted abruptly out of his elbow. Both these bones were badly splintered and the wounds in the skin where they came out were ugly and bleeding like hell. The machete had gone into his side just below the ribs and there was a gaping wound which was also bleeding heavily. His entire body was covered in smaller cuts and big black marks. The rest of him was as white as a new sheet.

'Holy shit!' I said to the amah. She nodded her head in tearful agreement. She loved us, that poor woman, and it really cut her up bad when things like this happened, and they happened an awful lot.

I went and got the brandy bottle, forced his lips open and managed to get a few drops in there. We had taken the precaution of installing a phone after the last couple of disasters, but my dear brother had managed to bring down the line with his tree, so I sent the amah down to the guardroom, telling her to get help: a Landrover, a medic and some soldiers. Then I set about the bulky part of the branch with the machete. I worked like a maniac but it was no good.

He must have been up there for hours to have cut through that damn thing. I tried to move it, but it weighed a ton and I feared I might crush Dave if I did manage to shift it even an inch.

At that moment the combined might of the British Army arrived to help – on foot, with our wailing, hair-pulling amah bringing up the rear – in the form of a solitary local NCO clutching a tube of aspirins and rolling his eyes. He took one look at Dave and fainted. I seriously thought about letting the dogs out to attack his remains, but just then the NAAFI motor scooter came pop-popping up the hill to deliver our groceries.

Before the guy even had a chance to dismount, I pushed him off and roared down the hill towards the kampong, leaving him stood there with open mouth. The scooter was his pride and joy. Luckily Richard Chan was there, and when he saw my devastated expression he asked no questions but just jumped on the pillion.

Back at the house nothing had changed. The NAAFI man was still stood in the middle of the road staring at the spot where his scooter had been. The NCO was still out cold on the grass. The amah was still crouched before Dave, wailing. Richard walked over to the felled branch, looked at Dave's battered body, looked back at me and shook his head.

'You guys,' he said. 'You guys.'

Then he crouched down and took the massive branch between his two arms and without so much as a grunt lifted it and threw it to one side. Jesus! I'd never seen anything like that.

I got some more brandy into Dave and he came round. He was very, very groggy, and started to lose more blood as he moved. I went in and got some shirts and TCP, then splattered the shirts with the stuff and wrapped them around the worst wounds as tight as I could. He must have been in agony, but he actually smiled at me and I could see he was game to come up with some suitable comment but couldn't quite manage it. We walked him slowly over to the motor scooter and sat him on the seat. Richard sat behind and held on to him tight, while I drove us back down the hill. On the jetty I commandeered the first army boat I saw. The Captain, a local, objected like hell, but I threatened to bust him in the mouth if he didn't get us to Jardine Steps pretty quick.

Richard was grinning like a madman on the boat ride, so I asked him what was so funny.

'You guys,' he replied, shaking his head. 'You guys . . . you guys are really out of order, you know that, don't you?'

I had to agree with him. I mean, the man had a very good point. He was right. We were totally one hundred per cent out of order.

I finally got the remains of my brother to the BMH in a taxi. The same doctor in casualty who'd treated his knife wounds took him in.

'Just who the hell are you guys?' he asked in some amazement at the broken and bruised body of my brother.

I didn't say anything.

'What happened to him for Christ's sake?' he persisted.

'Just a little disagreement,' I told him.

We never lost a chance to score points with our reputations. Dave was going under but he must have heard that one, because he bared his lips so you could see his big gold tooth shining.

'I'll get you . . . you bastard,' he whispered in dramatic style, and then faded away.

The doctor thought he had a real pair of hot potatoes on his hands and called the Military Police and I was 'extensively interviewed'. Richard Chan walked through one of the walls. One second he was there, the next he was gone. That was his normal reaction to people in Police uniform.

I wired the news to my parents in Malaysia a few days later when Dave was a little better.

'SORRY TO SAY DAVE INJURED IN ACCIDENT STOP IN BMH UNDER CONTROL STOP'

They wired back directly.

'WE KNOW STOP EXTENDING HOLIDAY FOR ANOTHER WEEK STOP'

I showed my brother the cable in his hospital bed.

'Ace!' he screamed. 'We can have a party.'

'You are diamond-tipped crazy, brother of mine. What are you talking about, a party?'

'You gotta organise everything. Promise! We are going to have the biggest God-damned party this pisspot country has ever seen!'

This broken boy in his hospital bed had vision. He laid it all out for me.

The doctors said that he would be inside for a month, at least, but he told me to forget that, he'd be there. One hundred per cent he'd be there. So I had to organise this visionary blow-out for the coming weekend. I was busy.

I got two live bands from my old school and arranged army launches to ferry the equipment across and Landrovers to carry the stuff up to the house. I moved all the furniture out on to the lawn with the help of Richard and friends. The smaller brothers watched all this in wide-eyed amazement from the safety of their bedroom doorway and really freaked out when we took their beds out and dumped them on the lawn. The smallest one said in his sweet little way, 'You are going to be in deep shit when they get back.'

I told him, 'Shut up. You'll get your ration of Tiger beer if you keep your mouth shut.'

He had a contract in his hand in twenty-two seconds and was shifting furniture once it was signed.

I went down to the floodlit badminton court at the Officers' Mess late at night and borrowed all their light fixtures and set them up in the garden. Then I walked into the NCO's bar as sweet as sugar and told the mess-manager that my father was throwing a party at the weekend and had sent me down to order forty cases of Tiger and they had better get it delivered fast. He did and I had to run around finding old bathtubs and things so I could ice the beer down in them.

There was no need to send out invitations. Once the rumour was out that the party of the century was about to take place on a certain little island you could guarantee a good turn-out. I made one rule: everybody had to bring a drink with them. Forty cases of Tiger would not go far in the mob we expected.

Dave arrived from the BMH, against the wishes of the doctors, having simply packed his stuff, walked out and got on a Changi bus for Jardine Steps. Wreathed in bandages and limping very badly, he could have passed as an extra for *The Curse of the Mummy's Tomb*. He looked over my work like a battlefield commander at Stalingrad and nodded his head in approval.

'You'd better invite Richard. We are bound to have trouble,' he said.

The simple, law-abiding residents of our island thought they were being invaded. From about midday, boats loaded down with undesirables started appearing at the jetty. After the twentieth boat our single Malay policeman put in a formal appearance and wanted to know what was going on. I reminded him that my father still had not settled up with him and that he wouldn't take too kindly to him poking his nose in my father's business. It was cool. He went away, happy to be of service. Some nervous neighbours hovered around in the distance but were scared off when the first band started up at around 3,000 watts. The noise was devastating. We started off counting the arrivals but gave up after 460. By nightfall I reckoned we had six hundred or more people crammed into our house and spilling into the garden. It was chaos. It was madness.

Dave strode about with two beer cans in his hands, shouting out, 'Great! Magic! Beers in the bathroom! Ace! Have a nice day, you bastards! Here's to Mr Lee Kuan Facking Yew!' and so on. I never saw anything so crazy. There were Boogey Street whores sitting down and shooting the shit with convent girls on holiday from England; local gangsters playing never-ending games of mah-jong for thousands of dollars on tables set up on the lawn; fishermen from the kampong staggering about clutching bottles of black rice wine and wishing all and sundry 'Happy New Year!' It was March, but who cares?

The youngest daughter of a very high-ranking RAF officer was stood on her head in the bathroom for two hours with no underwear on, giving anyone who wanted to look a biology lesson. It was disconcerting to be taking a piss when she was in the room like that.

I asked her, 'Are you happy like that?'

'Yeah,' she answered.

'I love you,' I said.

'You're the fourteenth,' she said.

'The fourteenth what?'

'The fourteenth to tell me that.'

'Oh.'

'I don't like boys anyway.'

'What do you like?'

'Can't you see?'

'Not really, no.'

'Standing on my head, you dipstick!'

'What about your pants?' I asked.

'Oh someone took them off about an hour ago.'

'Well, enjoy the party,' I said.

'I am,' she replied.

I always meet the most interesting people and have the most interesting conversations.

The bath was swimming with ice and cans of Tiger beer, but always had at least four people sitting in it. The smaller brothers wandered around with eyes as big as saucers clutching their ice-cold Tigers as per contract. This party was definitely their first experience of the facts of life, and they were loving it. I watched the youngest walk straight into a wall as if he thought there was a door there. He bounced off the wall and sat down on the floor, staring murderously at where he thought the door should be. The other one was following a girl around who had the most amazing tits and every time she stopped he spilt his beer down her dress and carefully wiped it off. Every room you walked into there was a couple furiously copulating on the floor or against the wall and people were shaking their cans and spraying them like they were dogs on heat. I wouldn't have liked to estimate how many convent girls lost their virginity that night . . .

The real dogs went around savaging anyone who dared to dance but were eventually thwarted by sheer weight of

47

numbers and took to protecting Dave from anyone who tried to get near him. A girl called Judith followed me around with nothing but her bikini bottom on. She had these real funny tits, all nipples, not big but long and thin – they stuck out in front of her by a good two inches. She never said anything, just followed me around with big doe-like eyes staring at me. She was crazy and had already had two abortions after twice letting some sailors gang-bang her. She was the grand old age of sixteen then. I set the dogs on her in the end and she ran off screaming, with them barking like hell, knocking drunks off into uncontrollable spins and taking bites out of anybody who got in their way. She was rescued by a couple of sixth-formers from my old school who took her outside for some serious discussion. They both got crabs.

At first we had one band play at a time, but after midnight they both played at the same time, trying to drown each other out with watts. One band got stuck like a scratched record with *Midnight Hour* by Wilson Pickett and played it over and over again. Groups of people were having gang fights – throwing empty cans, or shaking up full ones and spraying each other. Some guys started throwing bottles and I went over to discuss that behaviour with them.

'You shouldn't do that,' I said reasonably. 'People will cut their feet on the dance floor.' Nobody had shoes on. Most people had practically nothing on.

I knew these guys. There were off an RFA vessel, the *Tide Reach*, and we were friendly with them because they always gave us beer and a bit of dope now and again. They were friendly with us because it gave them the chance to sniff around a few schoolgirls.

A big fat one said, 'Fuck off, kid,' and threw a bottle against the wall.

Nobody was noticing this exchange. It was too hectic to notice anything.

I gave my special whistle and the dogs were at my feet in seconds.

'Listen. Why don't you be reasonable? If I tell these dogs to attack you, they will. We don't want no trouble with you guys. Just have a good time.'

Adults do not like fourteen-year-old boys telling them what to do, and these guys were no exception. Another bottle hit the wall. Then I saw the fat guy's eyes widen in surprise. They were looking at something behind me.

Now Richard had a good sense of humour. He also had that fantastic ability of the Malays for mimicry and acting, although he was only half Malay. I turned round to see him moving very slowly through the crowd of people, like a little Malay girl dancing in slow motion. His eyebrows were arched and his movements were fluid and feminine. He was dressed in the usual ragged trousers and nothing else. This was years before any of us had seen *The Incredible Hulk* but that is just what Richard looked like. His movements may have been feminine but his body was frightening seen in the flashing lights amid the mind-blowing music. His arm was bigger than my waist and the veins looked like blue express-ways. His torso rippled and glowed. Even to a friend he communicated animal menace in every girlish movement.

'What the hell is that?' the fat guy asked, dropping his bottle.

'I told you not to break any more bottles.' I informed him.

He bent down and started to pick up the pieces. When he came back up he was face to face with Richard. Richard put his hand out very slowly, took the guy's nose between thumb and forefinger, and gave it a good honk. Then he walked off laughing. Tears ran out of the guy's eyes.

'Shit! That hurt!' he exclaimed.

'Richard is the manager of this nightclub. He doesn't like people throwing glass about. OK?'

They all nodded their heads in agreement and I went back to the party. Richard was leaning against a wall and he gave me a big wink, then put away a can of Tiger. Richard was the coolest guy I ever met in my life.

From there on in the party went berserk. Dave wandered around in an alcoholic haze looking like a head-shot water-buffalo that someone had dug up out of a paddy field, dragging bandages around on the floor behind him and spilling his drink on anyone who cared to talk to him. People were rapidly turning into bodies that were dying on the floor in pools of Tiger beer and vomit. The bands played on and on. Someone had found an air rifle and was systematically shooting out the spots from the badminton court, while others threw cans of beer at him. There was a long queue of guys outside the toilet and when I pushed my way to the front and shoved the door open there was Judith gyrating about on the filthy floor with a guy trying to ride her for all he was worth. I said to the waiting guys, 'You'll all get crabs.'

'Who gives a shit!' they shouted in unison like a platoon of Marines. Judith was not drunk, that's the way she was all the time, even at school. I first met her in Religious Instruction when she sat down next to me and without any sort of formal introduction reached under the desk and unzipped the fly of my shorts and started fumbling about in there. I wanted to protest, but it's not too easy in the middle of Religious Instruction. I made sure I didn't sit next to her again, in any class.

The dogs were worrying something that resembled a sack of potatoes on the lawn. It was an old friend of mine from school and he was way over the top. The dogs had shredded his clothes but left his skin alone. I called them off and sent them on their perimeter patrol in case any police were hanging around. A girl threw herself off the balcony with a loud shriek as I walked past and stayed exactly where she had landed. I checked her pulse. She was still alive and didn't appear injured, just drunk. A group of people were crawling about on their hands and knees across the lawn and I thought it was some new game until I realised that they were all being sick. God! I wasn't feeling exactly one hundred per cent myself, so I staggered about the garden to try and sober up a bit.

An ex-convent girl called Jane grabbed me and hustled me into the privacy of the banana plants. She got her hands down the front of my shorts and just ripped them open. Buttons shot off into the night like small flying saucers.

'Christ, Jane! What the hell are you doing?'

She was normally very quiet and shy. The last time I had seen her was in the school library with all fourteen volumes of

A History of the English-Speaking Peoples by Winston Churchill in front of her.

'Shut up!' she screamed. 'Just *do* it to me, will you?'

'Do what to you?'

Her body went into overdrive and she was shaking like she had palsy or something. I thought, any moment now this person is going to start frothing at the mouth, and pushed her off. She grabbed my arm.

'Do it to me,' she said softly. She stopped shaking.

There was something about the way she said 'do' that cut me up. It hurt. I said, 'Ouch.'

'Why did you say "ouch"?' she asked.

'It hurts, your accent and when you say words like "do",' I explained.

She smiled, 'Dirty words you mean?'

'Yeah, dirty words.'

'I know a lot of dirty words.'

'Yeah?'

'What about fuck?' she asked.

'Ouch.'

She giggled, 'Big fat willies?'

'Ouch.'

'Ramming? Throbbing? Sticking it up? Juicy?'

'OK, OK, I'm convinced,' I told her.

'Good,' she said and took my shorts in her thumbs and pulled them down in one swift movement.

'I'm a virgin,' she announced.

'Christ,' I replied. It was my turn to shake.

'Lay down,' she ordered.

'Christ,' I said, but did.

She stood over me like the Statue of Liberty, then pulled her pants down and lay down on the ground with me.

'Make it go hard! Why isn't it hard?' she demanded.

'I don't know!'

'Well bloody well make it go hard!'

'I'm drunk. I am so drunk I think I have to vomit,' I told her.

'Please make it go bloody hard!'

'It won't . . . I'm drunk!'

51

'Jesus! Have I got to do everything? I never did this before. You're supposed to be the experienced one!'

'Who said so?'

'Never mind,' she said and started fiddling.

'It's still not hard!' she complained.

'I'm pissed out of my brain, for Christ's sake!'

'If it's not hard in ten seconds I'm going to give it away to someone else. Don't you want to do me?'

'I'm drunk!'

'Christ!' She jumped to her feet and crashed off through the banana plants. Her pants were still on the ground. I stuffed them into the pocket of my shorts, once I had them back on.

When I got back to the party some of the guys had taken all the furniture from the lawn and piled it all together like a crazy Sultan's palace: sofas, chairs, table, beds and wardrobes were all stacked up willy-nilly and reached about twenty feet in the air. At the top were some guys drinking beer and throwing empty cans at anyone who walked past. At other levels of the construction people were sleeping, copulating, laughing and crying. Another group came along and started pushing on the structure so it wobbled back and forth, but luckily it stayed standing. There was one guy, right at the bottom, crying his eyes out.

'What's wrong with you?' I asked him.

'She . . . she . . . ' he slobbered, 'she told me she was a virgin.'

'Who for Christ's sake?' I asked.

'Ju . . . Ju . . . Judith,' he sobbed.

'Ju . . . Ju . . . Judith?' I asked.

'Yeah . . . Ju . . . Ju . . . Judith.'

'You need your head read, my man,' I told him. 'Get the machinery adjusted.' I walked back into the bungalow. Judith a virgin? That was the joke of the year. And what was all this crap about virginity anyway? Christ! What a party. Inside was a disgusting mess of mostly dead bodies, but a few people were still attempting to dance. I leaned against the wall and watched them. Jane was there, dancing with some guy. He had his back to me so I couldn't recognise him. Then he

turned around. Thank you God! It was my old friend the
school bully, the underpants advert, Mr Perfect himself. I
started planning his fate directly. Let the dogs savage him?
Go up and simply kick him in the arse? Drown him in the
bath? Introduce him to Judith? But before I reached a
decision they stopped dancing and walked out onto the
balcony and down the stairs. I rushed after them and caught
Jane by the arm. She whirled round.

'What do you want?' she demanded.

'You forgot these,' I said, and took her pants out of my
pocket and handed them over to her.

Man! Did she go red.

I slapped the underpants advert around the shoulder, real
friendly.

'She goes like hell, my man, tightest box in Singapore,' I
said cheerfully. 'Hope you're up to it . . . filth.'

His jaw fell five inches and he gave her an evil look.

'You told me . . .' he started to say.

'That she was a virgin . . . ' I suggested, adding, 'filth.'

He nodded his head.

'She tells that to everyone, filth,' I said, and put my hand on
her dress and pulled it up over her hips. When he saw that
she was naked underneath he stomped off after snarling,
'Bitch!'

She looked at me for a whole of a second, then slapped me
very hard on the face.

'Bastard!' she hissed.

'It was worth it, darling,' I replied and walked back into the
party.

I was so pissed I was having the whirling pits. And I was
still upright! I couldn't take much more of this sort of shit so
had a look for Richard. He was playing mah-jong with some
gangsters on the back lawn. Dave was slumped in a seat
beside him with the dogs laying protectively around his legs.
He looked awful. I asked Richard if he could keep an eye on
things. He stopped shuffling stones for a second and looked
up at me.

'You guys,' he said, shaking his head, 'you guys.'

I crawled into my patch of banana plants and laid down.

My head was whirling and whirling, but if I kept still I reckoned I wouldn't be sick. There was a rustling and Jane's head loomed into my vision. She had a wicked grin on her face.

'Now I've got you, you little bastard!' she said, and started pulling my shorts down again.

'I'm drunk . . . can't move,' I mumbled.

She punched me in the stomach.

'*You* don't have to move!' she declared and that's the last thing I remember about that night.

It was supposed to be a two-day party but when I woke up at seven the next morning and surveyed the bruised and battered remains that had once been people, I came to the conclusion that nobody could sustain this type of shit over a forty-eight-hour period. It looked like a downtown Chicago Mafia massacre and I honestly expected to see Elliot Ness come walking in the door and say: 'Someone should inform the Mayor about this.'

Jane was laid on her back, snoring her head off, her skirt around her waist and ants crawling over her legs. I wondered whether we had managed to get rid of her troublesome piece of flesh. Somehow I doubted it . . . She'd tell me later anyway.

I wanted to shake my head as I walked around and took in the devastation, but my head felt like glue and if I moved too fast the world collapsed around me in a shower of glass that hurt real bad. The floors were a sea of Tiger beer and Tiger beer cans. The smaller brothers were curled up under some loudspeakers, their arms wrapped around each other, oblivious to the loud hum that was coming over the pa. The band were laid around their instruments as if someone had come in and zapped them all with a death ray. The dogs joined me in my survey, hoping for a walk down to the beach and a swim. No chance.

The gardens were in a hideous state. It looked like a Panzer division had just rolled out. The crazy tower of furniture was still standing – just. Survivors were strewn about in messy groups, motionless. A crow shouted from the breadfruit tree, the only sound . . . until I heard the noise of a motor making its way up the hill. I took no notice and went to look for Dave. I found him wrapped in his bloody bandages underneath a naked Judith in the bathroom. I gave him a gentle kick in the ribs. His eyes flickered open and he said, 'I got crabs.'

Then he went back to sleep.

The noise of the motor got louder. It stopped. I heard doors slamming and voices, so I walked round the side of the house expecting it to be some late guests. What I saw was the most horrifying thing I had ever seen in my life. There, without a shadow of a doubt, were my beloved parents, stepping out of an army minibus when they were supposed to be in the highlands of Malaysia. I was frozen to the spot with absolute terror. I watched my father's head come up with a smile on his face. The smile disappeared at a million miles per hour when he saw the tower of furniture piled up on the front lawn. My mother dropped her bag and fainted dead away on the spot.

'Jumping Jesus!' I swore to myself, and moved out of their line of vision very smartly.

As I passed Dave I gave him another gentle kick in the ribs. His eyes flickered again.

'Crabs ain't the only thing you got, brother of mine. Our folks just decided to pay us a surprise visit!' I told him.

5

Then I was gone. They could hardly beat my brother to death in his present state of health, and I had no doubt that he would lay the party well and truly on my doorstep. Couldn't blame him – I'd do the same to him. After all, that is what brothers are for. I won't say what happened but the repercussions of that evening are still going on now, twenty-two years later, and they are not very nice.

As usual I hid out in the kampong with Richard until father had sailed away to his southern battlefields, then moved back in with a mother who wasn't talking to me except to outline in murderous details what my father was going to do to me when he finally got his hands on my no-good body. Mother relented in the end – she always did, you can't stay in a state of war with your entire family for the rest of your life – and promised to try and convince father that we did have a better side. OK, it was hard to find, but it was there somewhere. I had to leave the house on the day he was due back, and as I was going down the hill he was coming up in a Landrover. His eyes swept over me as if I did not exist.

Mother sweet-talked him and he issued a general amnesty, the conditions of which were that we had to restore the house and garden to their former condition. Pocket-money was cancelled and placed into a fund to repair the furniture, and we had to swear on our mother's deathbed that we would be on our best behaviour at all times until we left Singapore. As my father put it, 'Once we get back to England I don't give a damn what any of you do, as I am throwing the whole lot of you out on your ears the minute that VC10 touches down.'

We managed to keep our side of the bargain for a considerable time; and then a riot intervened, a riot for which we were, at first, unfairly blamed.

It started out with a badminton match between some of the locals and us two older brothers. This was an event that took place every year and usually the locals won the match, no problem, but we'd been training with the British Army team, mainly because there was a bar at the badminton court and father had a bill there. We surprised everyone by thrashing every pair they put against us. The whole of kampong had turned out to watch the match, only Richard wasn't there . . . if he had been I know things would have turned out differently. By the time we'd inflicted a fourth defeat on their side, tempers were running high and the mood was getting ugly.

Apart from Dave and me, the only other English people there were the two small brothers, who were holding the dogs while we played. Dave had just put away a lovely smash into the back of the court when another player, who had been watching, ran on to the court and whacked him very solidly around the head with a badminton racket. It was such a vicious blow that the racket shattered and Dave went down like he had been hit with a stun-gun. I reacted quite normally under the circumstances, and with a restraint that I thought my father would have been proud of: I fetched that guy a beauty with my racket just below his right ear and he also went down like a stunned bull. Then all hell broke loose as the whole kampong invaded the court. About ten screaming guys engulfed me and started beating me with badminton rackets. I was whirling my racket around my head fending them off and throwing kicks at them, some of which connected satisfactorily. Dave was crawling off the court on his hands and knees with a load of guys kicking and thumping him as he went. The smaller brothers were trying to hold the struggling dogs by their collars.

'Let them go!' I screamed and they did.

Like blood-crazed furies the dogs tore into the crowd, slashing out with their teeth, and within seconds they had seriously injured about ten of the men. I got to Dave and pulled him up and staggered off with him while the dogs forced the crowd back. Someone threw firecrackers at the dogs and they ran back to us, allowing the crowd to surge forward again. A few of the men were waving machetes and the whole situation looked like it was rapidly turning revolutionary. The dogs behaved perfectly. Every time any of the crowd ran forward they attacked viciously, making them break and run. Then I looked to where the small brothers were and saw a group of men waving sticks and badminton rackets rushing up the small hill where they had taken refuge to watch the show.

I screamed to the dogs, 'There! There! Get them! Get them!'

The dogs stopped and looked around, confused. I let Dave drop to the ground.

'Get them!' I screamed and started running towards the smaller brothers. The dogs finally saw what I meant and went past me at a terrifying lick, their lips pulled back in horrible grimaces that showed their fangs. The men saw them coming, hesitated, then ran back down the hill. Still going full tilt, the first dog hit one of the men at shoulder height and knocked him flying. Then the other one had him as well, and they really ripped him up bad. I had my doubts as to whether he would live. I grabbed Dave, who was beginning to come around a bit, and shouted for the smaller brothers to join me, then we made our way slowly along the road towards the police compound at the other end of the kampong. The dogs joined us, with the crowd in full cry not far behind them. It was very tense, but with the police compound not far away they were hesitant about making a move. The single Malay policeman was at the gate of the compound looking very worried about the mob that was following us, waving sticks and machetes in the air and howling for revenge. At first he wouldn't open the gate – the compound was surrounded by a twelve-foot high fence – but I screamed at him, 'Open the bloody gate! I know you can understand English. Open it!'

With a great deal of reluctance he did. He obviously did not want to become the focal point of the crowd's anger. We sat down exhausted in the compound and the crowd clamoured around the fence, screaming insults and throwing rocks over the top. The hard core of them were trying to force their weight against the fence and break through, though the dogs kept up a constant attack on them through the fence. The policeman tried to lock himself in the small station house, but I prevented that by pushing the smaller brothers in after him. He then realised he was trapped.

'Get on your radio and call the guardroom for help!' I shouted at him.

He waved his hands in the air but didn't make a move to the radio.

'Do it!' I shouted.

He still did nothing.

'If they break in here, they will rip you apart as well as us. They are all Chinese. You are a Malay and a cop. They'll kill you.'

That convinced him and he radioed the guardroom. Luckily there was an English Sergeant on duty and he dispatched two Landrovers full of armed soldiers. Even when faced with that, the crowd didn't want to back down and kept on surging towards the compound. They knew the soldiers would never open fire. The English Sergeant came down himself in another Landrover. He was a giant of a man, well over six and a half feet and perhaps eighteen stone, and he walked around staring the men down until they broke up and moved a small distance away.

'Jesus!' he exclaimed when he saw the state of Dave and me. 'Your father is going to have your hides all right. Let's get you up to the guardroom where you'll all be a bit safer.' The Sergeant walked through the remaining crowd and three Landrovers followed with us in the middle one. At the guardroom he showed us into a big cell and locked the door.

'Considering the scale of the riot you boys caused, I'm keeping you locked up until I've spoken to your father and his Commanding Officer.'

So there we sat: two very bloody and bruised teenagers, two very frightened smaller brothers, and two exhausted but very brave dogs. I thought we all deserved a bloody medal.

My father, when he arrived six hours later, thought otherwise.

He looked at us through the bars for some minutes with his face getting redder and redder until I thought it would burst. The smaller brothers were removed before he gave vent to his feelings.

'Why?' he asked. 'Why did I have to have a pair of bastards like you two? Can you tell me what I have done to deserve this? Do you realise you have been responsible for creating the biggest riot this island has ever seen?'

He turned his back on us, obviously trying to control his temper. It failed. He spun round, grabbed the bars and shook them in his rage.

'Oh no! Wrecking my house and reputation is not good enough for you two bastards. You have to go one bloody step more, don't you? Do you realise that at this moment there is a Gurkha unit on its way here to try and defuse the situation you have created? A Gurkha unit for Christ's sake! My sons need the protection of a Gurkha unit! There are twelve people in the intensive care section of the BMH because of you bastards. The President of Singapore, Mr Lee Kuan Yew, has personally asked to be informed about your roles in this riot. I will probably be court martialled! My ship is leaving in two days time, and until then you two bastards stay right here. Why? Because if I could get my hands on you I would kill you. It's for your own protection. I've ordered the guard here to shoot your bloody dogs as well!'

'Over my dead body!' I shouted from the far corner of the cell where Dave and I were huddled together with the dogs, who were snarling viciously at father.

'With bloody pleasure!' snapped father, and then he was gone.

We were eventually exonerated by several locals, who came forward and said that we had been attacked and acted only in self-defence. Luckily the reprieve came in time to save the dogs. So we all lived.

Lived . . . but there were restrictions. We were not allowed to go down in the kampong, in case we got lynched and started another riot. Even mother, on strict orders from father, was not allowed out of the house. After a while Richard came up to the house and asked for me. Father glared from a distance as we spoke.

'Why haven't you been down to the kampong?' Richard asked.

I waved in father's general direction. 'He thinks we'll be murdered if we leave the house.'

Richard shook his head and laughed, 'You guys! It's OK for you and your family to come down to the kampong. Nobody, and I mean nobody, is going to give you any trouble, OK?'

'OK,' I said.

Richard walked off shaking his head and saying, 'You guys . . . You guys . . . '

'What did he want?' asked father.

'Er, well, he said it's OK for us to go out, to go down to the kampong and stuff like that.'

'Jesus! I don't believe this family. I don't believe this at all. You bastards start the biggest riot this island has ever seen. My Commanding Officer tells me that I have to keep my family safe at home, where we have Gurkhas protecting us, and then you, YOU get a visit from one of the biggest gangsters in Singapore and he tells YOU that it's safe for my family to leave the house. That is it! That is the limit!'

He stormed off in disgust, but deep inside he knew that when Richard said we wouldn't have any more trouble, we wouldn't have any more trouble. That was the problem with Richard Chan, he was too bloody good to be true.

6

Richard Chan . . . If I close my eyes hard and concentrate, the clouds of alcohol recede and I can see him walking towards me in some crazy backstreet with the crowds of shouting Chinese parting before him, two fighting cocks tied around his neck by their feet and bouncing on his bare chest, that strange smile playing over his face . . . I can feel the sand under my bare feet and in my hands the tight electric power of a fighting bird waiting to be let go. The noise from the crowd is deafening . . . Then it all cuts to grey again and I'm back in this stinking hotel room staring at a bottle of gin. That really gets me angry. It's an empty bottle of gin. Out of the window I can see my old island. Perhaps Richard is still there, perhaps I can just hike out of here and take a walk into the past – close the door on this rancid, no-hope future and get the hell out of here. Richard would be an old man now, very old, maybe even a very dead old man. What the hell! I get another forty-dollar bottle of gin out of the fridge and phone the desk.

'Do you know the island that used to be a British Army base?' I ask.

'Sure, Sir,' he answers, 'It's a Singapore Navy base now.'

'I want to visit some people on the island, old friends of mine, can you tell . . . '

He interrupts me, 'There are no people on the island, only the sailors,' he says, 'and it's forbidden to visit the island anyway.'

'Forbidden! What do you mean forbidden? What do you mean there's no people?'

'The island was depopulated, Sir, when the British left.'

I threw the phone across the room. What a word! *Depopulated*. You wait, you just wait, Mr Lee Kuan Facking Yew, till I get my hands on you. I should have kicked you in the balls in 1967. The guy was still squawking on the phone so I pulled myself together and picked it up again.

'Is it possible to trace someone who lived on the island once?' I ask.

'Very unlikely, Sir, after all this time.'

'Thanks.'

I hung up with a little more tact. I have to be a very unusual person. I mean, who else has friends who get depopulated? Still, if I know Richard he probably lit out of this stinking country years ago and is running a mah-jong house in San Francisco or somewhere . . . After all this time.

I close my eyes again and feel the warm sand beneath my feet. Overhead, lightning-bright, pumped-up kerosene lanterns throw a shadowless glaring wave of light over the heaving crowd of Chinese, who are screaming their heads off and waving wads of dollars in the air. It's a madhouse, maybe five hundred people slammed into this airless ghost of a shed. The place stinks of shit, Tiger beer and sweat, in that order. I'm the only white person in this seething pit of yellow, shining faces.

Richard touched my arm. 'You know what to do?' he asked.

I nodded my head, making sweat run into my eyes. It must have been a hundred degrees in there.

Crouching in the sand, on the other side of the ring, was a Chinese guy holding a savage-looking fighting cock between his hands. I unstrung the birds from around my neck and gave one to Richard, then knelt down in the sand with the other bird, opposite the Chinese guy. Using my teeth I undid the twine holding the bird's legs together, then held the bird up so he could see his enemy. The birds bristled directly, neck feathers up proud, claws scrabbling the air. In their eyes was the red look of absolute madness that only fighting cocks can get when they see an opponent. Between my hands I could feel his muscular, taut little body expanding and contracting with an evil, electric anger. I looked up at Richard, leaning against the side of the ring, and he winked. It was cool.

The Chinese let his pent-up ball of fury loose and Richard shouted, 'Now!'

Normally fighting cocks dance around each other for a while, sizing one another up, but this little murderous bird of Richard's tore straight into the other, raking savagely with his natural claws – we never put spurs on the birds – and feathers burst into the air like someone had ripped a pillow apart. Twenty seconds later the other bird was laid on the sand, panting and bloody. Richard gave me the whistle to grab our bird and I neatly caught it and tied its legs back together. Suddenly a big fat Chinese burst into the ring and started screaming insults at me. He was naked from the waist, and massive, with a belly that could have swallowed me and still had room for a polar bear or two. Sweat poured down his face and dripped onto his chest. In his hand was a great wad of dollars which he waved at me while calling me every pig, dog, camel, vulture and sonofabitch that lived under the sun. He had obviously lost a lot of dollars on the wrong bird and was gibbering with rage.

There is something about the Chinese that makes them go completely bananas sometimes. They flip out over nothing and a person has to be very careful. Many times I'd been sat in some dirty downtown Chinese eating house enjoying a quiet *maa-mee* when the cook would burst into the room waving a big meat axe and attack a table of customers. Then the customers were just footprints in the grease and you could hear the enraged bellows of the cook as he chased them down the street. They had probably complained about the sauce or something. When the mood is on them the Chinese think nothing of stabbing, shooting or hacking someone into little pieces, and this gigantic Chinese stood in front of me looked like he was just about ready to rip my arms off and beat me around the head with them. I was one hundred per cent terrified. I shouldn't have been.

Richard glided between us like a ballet dancer and looked up at the guy – his head didn't even come up to his chin. The guy kept on screaming even though anyone with even a sand grain of sanity in their head could've seen that Richard was a loaded gun just waiting for some pumpkin to pull the trigger. Sure enough, Richard's right hand shot out like a striking cobra and he slapped the man, once, twice, around the face. The reports were like rifle shots and the fat guy's eyes actually rolled around in his head like marbles. The deafening clamour from the crowd dropped away to silence. Nobody moved, nobody breathed. It was as if the whole shed had suddenly sucked its breath in and was holding it. Richard's hand shot out again. CRACK! CRACK! This time the guy's head swung back at a sickening angle, his jaws gaped open and he rocked slowly back on his heels, tottered and then went down like twenty bags of cement with a big *whumph* in the sand. When Richard hit someone, even when it was only a playful slap, you could see it hurt real bad. God knows what would have happened if he'd actually punched someone. Richard bent down and took the wad of dollars from where they'd fallen on the sand and stuffed them into his pocket.

That was the first time he took me to a cock fight, and I soon found out that a little disagreement like that was nothing. Another time we were watching a cock fight when this well-dressed Chinese dude came screeching into the ring, pulled out a huge revolver and let one of the birds have it with a full magazine: BLAM! BLAM! BLAM! The explosions were deafening and the poor bird was blown to hell and back. The whole crowded shed erupted into pandemonium, screaming people scrambling over seats and each other in a frenzy to get to the exit. I threw myself under my seat – the maniac with the insane grin on his face and the smouldering gun in his hand was only about five feet away from me. Richard stayed exactly where he was. When the guy had gone, I climbed out of my hiding place and sat down by Richard. He wagged a finger in front of my face, 'If he did that to one of my birds I would kill him,' he told me very seriously.

After a cock fight it wasn't unusual for the police to fish various bodies and parts of bodies out of the harbour. Without Richard around I couldn't have gone within a mile of one. It was the same with the big mah-jong games: strangers were not welcome. But I used to sit there all night, drinking Tiger beer and watching Richard gamble thousands of dollars. Sometimes he won, but only sometimes. The sound of mah-jong stones being shuffled late at night in the dark depths of the kampong is probably the strongest memory I have of Singapore.

The island is just out of the window, so near but gone forever. I can see the small hill where the old water tower was, where I lived like a savage with my dogs for nearly six months. It was a long time ago that I was leaping about on the top of that tower with the two dogs, howling and screaming at the best sunset I ever saw. When we first arrived in Singapore my parents said, 'We are having no pets this time, and that's final!'

I didn't take us long to break that little rule.

7

Our old colonial bungalow was infested with rats, absolutely heaving with the beasts. They used to run around in the ceiling space like a horde of Mongol warriors, dig their way up through the wooden floors, play catch across the living room, and float around in the monsoon drains on their backs wearing sunglasses.

We used to write mother little messages and leave them as book marks in her latest novel, stuff like: 'Even the ancient Egyptians understood that if you have a cat in the house, you have no rats.'

Or we'd sit in the living room armed with air rifles and blast the little buggers as they scampered in through the door. But mother was adamant, even when Dave pointed out to her that three rats were sitting in front of the television watching the latest episode of *The Lone Ranger*. We had given up any hope of ever getting a cat when our corpulent neighbour came to the rescue.

We were having a typical lazy afternoon, drinking father's Tiger beer and throwing the empty cans at the rats, when a gibbering, hysterical amah arrived under full steam with the usual hair-pulling, wailing and breast-beating. She was in remarkable form even for an amah, and we watched her in wide-eyed amazement for at least ten minutes before we notified mother of her presence. Dave announced, 'Mother, there is a hysterical amah in the room.'

She put her book down and gazed at the quivering form stood right in front of her.

'Oh dear,' she said.

We knew she worked for the neighbour, but we couldn't find out what she wanted. She just howled in a demented manner and pointed in the direction of our neighbour's house. Even our own amah could get no sense out of her, so we marched over to the house. As we neared it the amah's howling intensified and as if in reply someone shrieked back very loudly from the house.

We were impressed by this performance, and half expected to walk in on a full-scale bloody massacre, Indonesian communists disembowelling harmless army wives, raping attractive amahs' daughters, beheading gardeners, etc. The amah didn't need to guide us, the shrieking was very obviously coming from the bathroom. We all stood outside the door and listened. Mother knocked boldly on the door and called out, 'Mrs James? Are you quite all right?'

Dave and I rolled our eyes at one another.

'Of course she's not all right, mother,' Dave said, testily, 'she wouldn't be screaming like a stuck pig if she was all right.'

'She's probably singing,' I added.

The shrieking continued unabated.

'Whatever shall we do?' mother asked.

'*We* are doing nothing, mother,' Dave told her. '*You* are going in there to see what is going on.'

Mother looked shocked.

'Me! Why should I go in there?' she demanded.

'Mrs James might be naked, mother,' I replied.

'And it would not be very good for the moral education of your sons to be exposed to the sight of a fully mature naked woman,' Dave added in a most serious fashion.

Mother was quite sensitive about our moral education, if not our real education.

'Yes, quite right,' she said. 'I shall go in there.'

She knocked on the door again and called out, 'Mrs

James? Do not be alarmed. I am coming in.'

The shrieking intensified.

Very nervously mother tried the door handle.

'Oh God! It's not locked,' she said, with obvious disappointment.

'Get on with it, mother!' we both insisted.

She pushed the door open a fraction and peered around the edge, then quickly slammed it shut again.

'Oh God!' she exclaimed.

'Well! What is it?' we both demanded.

'Mrs James . . . she . . . she is sitting in the bath and shrieking,' she answered.

'She must be screaming for some reason. You have to go right into the room and see what is going on,' Dave said.

'Go on, mother. Get on with it,' I urged.

She pushed the door open and slid through. Two seconds later the door flew swiftly open and mother came running out, shrieking as well.

'Jesus!' Dave shouted, and grabbed her before she could get away.

'Well mother. What is it?' we demanded when she had calmed down a few moments later.

'Oh God . . . It's awful. That poor woman . . . Terrible. Oh God, that poor woman. There is a . . . a . . . a rat,' she managed to get out.

'A rat?' I asked.

She nodded her head.

'In the bath,' she said.

'In the bath?' Dave and I exclaimed.

She nodded her head again.

'Mrs James is also in the bath,' she added unnecessarily.

I looked at Dave and he looked at me and we both fell over on the floor, doubled up, with tears streaming out of our eyes.

'A rat!' Dave screeched.

'In the bath!' I shouted back.

'With . . . with . . . '

I was hooting with hysterics. 'With Mrs James!' I finished.

Mother stood over us, furious.

'It's not funny!' she shouted.

Dave pointed at her, cackling like a madman. 'Not funny she says!' He rolled over onto his knees.

'Get up! The both of you, this minute! One of you has to go in there and help that poor woman!' she sternly told us. 'Pull yourselves together for heaven's sake!'

We slowly got up. Dave was shaking his head.

'Oh no, mother,' he said. 'Oh no. I'm not going in there with a naked woman and a rabid rat. Oh no.'

'One of you has to! The wretched animal is swimming in circles around Mrs James and keeps trying to climb out of the water using her body. It looks like it has bitten her several times already. She probably tried to beat it away with her hands, poor thing.'

Dave pointed at me. 'He's the animal expert. He can do it.'

Mother gave me an appraising glance. 'Yes. Dave is quite right, you do have a way with animals.'

'Mother! I may have a way with animals but a mad rat in the bath of a very large and hysterical Englishwoman is altogether something different,' I told her in no uncertain manner. I was not frightened of the rat. It was the sight of a naked Mrs James that terrified me. She was definitely not peep-show material.

'You'll do as you are told, young man!' Mother said emphatically.

Dave nodded his head in agreement.

'Shit!' I said.

'Don't use language like that! Now go in there and do something to help Mrs James!' Mother ordered.

'All bloody right,' I agreed reluctantly. 'But I say it again, *shit*!'

I started to push the door open.

'Wait a minute,' mother said, and rushed off. When she came back she had a towel in her hand. 'You will have to wrap that around your head before you go in,' she told me.

'Whatever for?' I asked.

'I can't have you looking at Mrs James when she is not dressed,' she answered primly.

'Good God!' I snarled.

Dave was grinning happily, so I gave him a good just-you-wait-till-later look.

Mother wrapped the towel tightly round my head and then they pushed me through the door. Needless to say, I couldn't see a thing.

'Mrs James,' I shouted out. 'I've come to help you.'

Rather than calming her down, the sight of a young man with a towel wrapped around his head in her bathroom sent her off to even greater heights of hysteria. At least the appalling noise allowed me to find the bath. I touched the edge and was about to start searching about for the rat, which I could hear swimming frantically around the bathtub and squeaking to itself, when I had a horrible thought: What if I actually touched a naked part of Mrs James? This would be far worse than seeing her naked, I reasoned. The very thought made my flesh creep. So I took the towel off my head.

What a sight! Mrs James was E bloody NORMOUS. She obviously never went out in the sun as her skin was white as dough, and to set it off her mountainous body was topped with a ridiculous pretty-pink bathing cap. I tried not to look too closely at her, but there was no avoiding her gigantic breasts, bouncing up and down as she splashed the water with her hands in an effort to keep the rat at the other end of the bath. Her eyes were fixed on a point somewhere on the ceiling, and when I looked up I saw a small hole in the plaster through which the rat must have made its spectacular entry into the bath. The rat was a monster, and clearly could not escape from Mrs James' bath because of the smooth porcelain sides.

I could see why the rat couldn't get out of the bath, but I saw no reason why Mrs James shouldn't simply climb out and solve the problem herself.

'Mrs James,' I said. 'Get out of the bath. Jump out and you'll be OK!'

She continued to shriek and splash the water with her hands, and since her eyes were still staring up at the ceiling it was obvious she was not receiving my signals. If you can't get the woman out of the bath, then get the rat out, I thought. I dropped the towel into the water and let it hang over the side of the bath. The rat swam directly for it and climbed out with obvious relief. He shook the water off his fur, gave me what looked like a very grateful look, and then ran around the bathroom trying to find a way out. Mrs James continued to splash the water and shriek. I opened the door and the rat ran out, collided with mother's legs – causing a fresh outburst of screaming from her – and then raced off to the safety of the garden.

'Phew!' I said. 'It's all yours, mother.'

Dave and I left mother to cope with Mrs James. Her screams had not lessened one bit, even though the rat was probably back in his hole by now, telling his buddies that he'd seen the Day of Judgement and it was not a pretty sight.

'Bastard,' I said to Dave in the garden.

He held out his hands in front of his chest, encompassing an imaginary gigantic bosom, and danced around in front of me.

'Were they honeydew or water melons?' he asked.

'Bastard,' I said again, then added, 'The biggest water melons you ever saw in the whole of your miserable little life.'

'Yeehaa!' he shouted and scampered off, with me in hot pursuit.

Mrs James was flown back to England a few days later, never to return.

But we got our cat. Mother was convinced we needed one after Mrs James' horrifying experience. So I kidnapped an evil ginger tom from a Chinese family in the kampong. That thing had character. He'd kill twelve rats in ten minutes and then sleep it off in the fridge. He even used to drink Tiger beer, and when drunk he could have torn apart an angry wolverine. We called him Shitbag.

Father came home from his war and was sat nursing a whisky when Shitbag struggled backwards into the room with the disembowelled carcass of a huge rat in his mouth.

'What is *that*?' Father demanded.

'A cat, dear,' mother replied.

'A *cat*!?'

'Yes dear, a cat.'

'It looks more like a bloody panther to me.'

'It's a very good ratter, dear.'

'I can bloody well see that!'

'Its name is Shitbag,' I offered.

He threw me a glance that would have frozen a polar bear dead in its tracks.

So we had our cat. The next step was to get our dogs. I knew this wasn't going to be easy as my father had a pathological hatred of dogs stemming from when he was set upon by a pack of army guard-dogs in Gibraltar. Mother wouldn't even discuss the subject, so it was left to me to come up with something devious.

Our old bungalow occupied the remotest location of all the army houses on the island, right on the edge of the dense jungle that covered half the island. The nearest neighbour, now that Mrs James had fled, lived half a mile away, and at night the old bungalow was a lonely and spooky place. Dave and I shared a room, the smaller brothers had another and the parents' bedroom was on the other side of the house. I waited until father had gone away for his regulation three months' 'confrontation' duty, then sneaked out of bed one night at two in the morning, crept out of the house, raced round to mother's bedroom window and ran my hand noisily up and down the wooden shutters, then raced quickly back to my room. I had just thrown the covers over myself when the door burst open and in charged mother in full battle order, clutching the oversized wooden spoon she had won for poorest shot in the Women's Rifle Club.

'Quick!' she shouted, waving the spoon wildly about in the air. 'There's someone outside trying to break in.'

We both shot out of bed and went outside to investigate.

'There's nothing there, mother,' Dave said, after our futile search. 'You must have imagined it.'

She shook her head.

'I heard someone out there. They were trying to get in my window.'

We calmed her down and sent her back to bed after leaving most of the outside lights on at her insistence. Each night I organised something similar: mysterious noises, objects being moved about in the garden overnight, rattles, shrieks, and so on. Soon I had the whole family in a state of extreme agitation, convinced that the house was surrounded every night by gangs of thieves and desperadoes. The army put in an appearance occasionally but it was easy enough to work around them.

Mother often brought the subject of these mysterious disturbances up at the dining table, and I would always say something like, 'If we had some dogs, this sort of thing wouldn't happen you know, mother.'

The three brothers would nod their heads in collective agreement, but mother's head continued to shake in a negative fashion.

So I planned something spectacular for the night before my father's return from Borneo. I bought a six-foot string of powerful Chinese firecrackers and a long length of twisted paper fuse from a small shop in the kampong. After dark I put them in the tree midway between the smaller brothers' and mother's bedroom and ran the fuse back to my own room. Everyone was too busy watching the television to notice. I waited until two o'clock in the morning to make sure Dave was sound asleep, then crept over to the window with a box of matches. Dave and I never closed our shutters as we had the cat in our room to keep the rats at bay, so it was an easy matter to lean out without making a lot of noise and find the fuse. I struck the match and was just about to apply it to the fuse when Dave suddenly sat up in bed and asked, 'What the hell are you doing? Smoking?'

Before I could reply he jumped out of bed and ran over to me. He looked down at the fuse in my hand.

'What are you doing, you idiot?' he demanded.

'Er . . . Well . . . I . . .'

He looked out of the window but it was too dark to see the bundle of firecrackers. However, there was no mistaking that the fuse in my hand ran out of the window into the garden.

'Come on, out with it!' he demanded again.

'Firecrackers,' I said.

'Firecrackers?' he echoed.

'Yes. Firecrackers,' I replied.

'You are planning to blow us all up as we sleep, is that it?'

'Well, no . . . Not blow up, no. Just a little explosion,' I explained.

'I think father is right. You are bloody crazy.'

'Dogs,' I said.

'Dogs?'

'Yes, dogs.'

'What about dogs?' he asked.

'Don't you see?'

'No, I don't bloody well see!'

'Mother will let us have some dogs,' I explained.

He went and sat down on his bed.

'So, you are the one responsible for driving us all half crazy for the last three months. You really are mad. Don't you realise that mother is about two inches from a nervous breakdown?'

'Dogs,' I repeated.

'You have no morals whatsoever.'

'Dogs.'

I knew he wanted a dog as much as me. He sat lost in thought for a long time.

'Do you really think it's going to work?' he asked.

I nodded my head.

'Light the bloody thing then,' he said.

'No. I know you. You'll tell,' I said. I held the matches out to him. 'You light the bloody thing.'

He looked hard at me, but not for long.

Ten seconds later there was a series of terrific bangs as the string of powerful crackers ignited.

Father arrived to find mother in a state bordering on madness, convinced that there had been a Triad shoot-out in the garden during the night. During a frantic discussion about security, Dave and I both voiced the opinion that if we had a couple of good dogs this sort of thing wouldn't happen and father could go away without having to worry about the fate of his brood. After all, we pointed out, he was hardly ever there, so it was unfair that we should all have to suffer these night-time disturbances just because he didn't like the idea of dogs in the house.

The dogs were approved the same day.

Finding the dogs was no problem. The kampong was crawling with mangy curs and it was there that I had been looking out for suitable specimens for some months. I had found a whole family of particularly vicious brutes that lived in the vicinity of one of the curry shops. One of the bitches had whelped four months previously, and produced three fine looking pups, all jet black except for a white flash on the chest. I had already been feeding these half-grown dogs for a month, and within a short time had gained the confidence of the two I wanted. With slow wags of their tails they simply followed me home. I took the sensible precaution of making sure father was away again before bringing them to the bungalow. I knew he would take one look at them and the canine permit would be cancelled forthwith.

They were a filthy pair of twins, covered in sores and scabs. One had half an ear missing, the other had a hole where its right eye should have been. Neither would have ever won a cuddly dog contest, but that was not the quality I was looking for. They were big, lanky, ferocious brutes and great battlers amongst the kampong dogs. Mother was not impressed.

'What on earth are those things?' she asked when I told her to come outside and see her new bodyguards.

'Dogs, mother.'

'I can see that! I thought we were going to have a nice golden retriever or something,' she complained.

Dave came out to look at my brutes.

'Wow!' he exclaimed.

'Mother, the idea was to have guard-dogs. I'll train these dogs up so that anyone coming within one hundred yards of the house will be ripped to pieces,' I explained.

'Wow!' Dave said again. 'I want the one with only one eye!'

'I'm sure it's not really necessary to have them ripping

people to pieces on the lawn. It will be quite sufficient if they bark or something like that,' mother said.

'Yes, mother,' I replied.

'And you are not to bring them inside until they are clean and house-trained.'

'Yes, mother.'

Dave said, 'Rape and Pillage!'

Mother gave him a strange glance, 'I beg your pardon?' she asked.

'That's what we'll call them, Rape and Pillage. Great!'

On the whole the dogs worked out for the best. They had some minor faults – like a deep mistrust of father because he wasn't there when I first brought them home. In fact they attacked him in great style when he came back for the first time. Luckily both Dave and I were on hand and father escaped with only ripped uniform trousers, savaged hat and a dent in his pride. But they were very loyal to the rest of us, and eventually even grudgingly accepted father as an occasional visitor to the household. We certainly were not troubled by any midnight prowlers after their arrival. Mother commented on this to father at the dinner table one day.

'The dogs have certainly worked out well, dear. No disturbances at all since we got them. I sleep so much better now.'

Dave and I smiled at each other over the table.

Father grunted, then said, 'That may well be so, but I do not like the way their bloody evil eyes follow my every movement. It makes me feel like a stranger in my own house.'

He ate for a while, then put his cutlery down, looked along the table at all of us for a few moments, then shook his head slowly. 'I sometimes think it would be better if I were a stranger here. I'm convinced that every last single one of you is insane. Rape, Pillage and Shitbag. That just about sums up my family.'

8

No, I didn't feel guilty about how I got the dogs. What the hell! As far as I was concerned no self-respecting kid would spend four years on a beautiful tropical island without a pair of good dogs to share in the adventures. Thank God I didn't have to go to school any more, that would have been criminal.

I suppose I should also feel guilty about how my parents suffered in those days, but I don't, because most of it was accidental. OK, the party was no accident, but just about everybody has an illegal party when they are young. Our party was perhaps a little over the top but that was our style. As Richard always said, 'You guys!'

The next great event after the party and the riot landed me in hospital. Dave was practically insane with jealousy, because I had even managed to top his suicide act.

Rabies.

When my father was told he said, beaming all over his face, 'I knew it. I knew it couldn't all be my bloody fault.'

Fourteen days I had to stay in an isolation ward where huge sadistic nurses stuck enormous needles into my stomach, telling me it wasn't going to hurt a bit when it hurt like hell. Meanwhile the army had a kampong dog chained up and were waiting to see if it would start frothing at the mouth. The dog had attacked me in the middle of the kampong. My own dogs had been with my brother on an expedition somewhere else on the island, and this gaunt, half-starved shadow of a dog had taken advantage of the situation and ripped chunks out of my arms and legs in a savage attack which I eventually stopped by holding his jaws apart with my hands until he started howling and then ran off. The soldiers caught him later and chained him up.

The dog did not develop rabies but the soldiers shot it anyway and I was allowed to go home. When I got back I used to wait until late at night, then put shaving foam around my mouth and scare the hell out of the smaller brothers by throwing myself on the floor of their bedroom and thrashing about like a rabid dog. Mother eventually stopped me doing that. But later the brothers were very proud and used to tell all their friends that their crazy brother had rabies. They would always ask me when they had a visitor, 'Come on! Do your rabies act.'

It was about this time that I started to become really strange – content to be on my own with the dogs and not really wanting contact with anyone. I didn't even see much of Richard, and for once was following his advice and staying well away from girls. He was always telling me how girls were bad for the health, but I never believed him. Up till then I'd always found them bloody marvellous for the health. Talking about girls, I just remembered the time when mother tried to explain the facts of life to Dave and me. That was great.

Mother didn't often drink, but for some reason this one night she really hit the gin bottle and was sprawled in her bamboo chair gibbering to herself and laughing her head off. We were not ones to miss an opportunity, and laid into the fridge, wolfing down Tigers like you wouldn't believe. We were probably costing my father a dollar a minute. After an hour of heavy drinking we decided to steal mother's gin bottle. We sneaked on our hands and knees into the living room where mother was drowning herself in gin and babbling and cackling to herself. Every so often she would let rip with a hysterical shriek of laughter. This had frightened the smaller brothers so much that they locked themselves in their room. The smallest one peered out at Dave and me crawling across the floor towards mother's gin bottle.

'You are all loonies!' he said and slammed the door.

Mother saw Dave just as he was about to grab the bottle.

'That's my gin, you little sod!' she said and slapped his hand away.

We decided to have a dog-fight in the dining room instead. Dave had Rape at one end of the room and I was on the other side with Pillage.

'Kill! Kill!' screamed Dave holding his struggling dog by the collar.

'Kill! Kill!' I screamed back, holding my brute.

Then we let them go. They tore into each other with blood-curdling growls, their hackles vertical and teeth flashing, scattering bamboo furniture all over the place and sliding in a snarling, slashing heap across the marble floor. Although the fight looked really vicious we knew they wouldn't hurt each other. It was a game we often played with them.

'Kill cat!' Dave screamed and they stopped fighting directly, leaped up on their paws and looked madly about for the cat. Then they were off, paws skidding on marble and howling like demons. They crashed into the living room with us not far behind, where mother was still gibbering to herself, and attacked Shitbag, who was sleeping on the sofa. That evil tom was no newcomer to this game and reacted like the little stick of dynamite he was, exploding off the sofa in a spitting ball of fury and landing right on top of Rape's head, which he scratched and raked with all four sets of talons. Pursued by Pillage they charged blindly round the room, Shitbag hanging on for grim death, crashing into furniture and bouncing off walls. Then the cat let go, made a sudden dash for the sofa, and did several rapid circuits around it with the two dogs hot on his tail. Finally, the whole screaming, howling, hissing mob disappeared out of the balcony door, direction: jungle.

Mother had carried on sipping her gin and staring into the glass during the whole mêlée. We were just about to walk out when she said, 'Boys.'

We sat on the sofa and looked at her. Her glasses were nearly falling off and she looked like she was well and truly

80

bombed. She was holding the glass at such an angle that the gin was dripping slowly onto the floor.

'Boys,' she said very solemnly, 'I have something to say to you.'

'Yes, mother,' we both said.

She stared directly at us but we could tell her eyes were focussing on another planet. Two minutes passed.

'Well?' Dave demanded finally.

Her eyes came back to us.

'It's about time . . . ' she said, and then her eyes wandered off again. We waited and waited but nothing else came.

'Shall I get you another gin, mother?' I asked. The glass was empty and there was a puddle of gin around her feet. The sound of my voice seemed to click her back into place.

'It's about time . . . Yes, it's about time,' she said once again.

'What's about time, for God's sake, mother?!' Dave shouted.

'Your father thought so . . . and I think so as well. It's your age, you see. Well, Dave is nearly sixteen now, or is it the other one . . . ' Her voice faded away and she was gibbering to herself again.

We looked at one another, shook our heads, got up and walked out of the room. As we got a beer from the kitchen we could still hear her voice droning on and on. We sat on the balcony and watched Rape and Pillage chase Shitbag one way around the house and then Shitbag chase Rape and Pillage around the other way.

'I think she has finally blown her fuses,' I offered.

'Your fault,' Dave replied.

'Why is it my fault?'

'You put the iguana under the table at breakfast.'

'Ah, she's used to that by now,' I said. 'I reckon it's your fault.'

'Why me?'

'When you died, she never got over that, you should have seen her rolling about on the grass and screaming out "Dave! Dave!" '

'At least I never got rabies,' he replied. 'I'm going in to see what she's on about now.'

He was laughing when he came back.

'She is still talking to us, I think,' he said. 'Something about school and she's worried that they might not have explained it properly or something. Christ only knows what she is jabbering about. You go and have a listen and bring two beers back with you, and her gin bottle if you can get it off her.'

She was slumped back in her chair with a serene and gentle smile on her face, talking in a melancholy manner that I'd never heard before.

' . . . and of course it is different for girls. They're not like boys, are they? It was the same when I was a girl as well. Boys should know these sort of things, shouldn't they?'

She nodded her head in agreement with herself.

' . . . and of course until I met your father I was a virgin.'

Wow! This was getting hot. I shouted out to Dave to get his act into the room double quick. We sat on the sofa opposite her.

'Yes . . . a virgin. Of course other men tried' – here she wagged a finger in the air – 'but I kept my legs closed!'

We applauded and whistled.

'More, mother!' Dave shouted.

'You should know that,' she said, trying desperately to fix us with a stern glance; but it slid off her face along with her glasses and landed on the floor. 'Good girls keep their legs closed . . . until the honeymoon. It is only proper . . . I wanted you to know that.'

Her eyes finally closed and she slumped back in her chair, dead to the world.

'I think mother has just explained the facts of life to us,' Dave announced.

'It's a thrilling thought, isn't it?'

'What?'

'That if mother had kept her legs closed we wouldn't be here.'

Dave looked at me for almost a minute. Finally he said, 'I

somehow think that when father looks at us lot he bloody well wishes that she had kept her legs closed.'

We shook hands on that one and Dave went and got a couple more beers. We swigged them and looked at mother's comatose form.

'How old were you?' Dave asked.

'What?'

'The first time, you know?' he explained.

'Eleven,' I said.

'Eleven! Christ! Who the hell was that? Not Cynthia?'

I laughed, 'No, Cynthia was number two. It was that German girl who lived in our block of flats in Hong Kong.'

His mouth fell open and he dropped his can of beer on the marble floor where it lay gently frothing. Shitbag appeared from nowhere and started lapping it up.

'Impossible!' he said. 'She was seventeen for Christ's sake!'

'Eighteen,' I corrected him.

He shook his head.

'No, no . . . I don't believe it. Eleven-year-old boys do not lose their virginity to eighteen-year-olds. Imagination and ability – you are mixing them up again.'

'It's true. She took me behind the flats and did things to me, then let me do things to her. It was the day we all went and had cholera injections and had no school. I'll tell you one thing, she explained things a hell of a lot better than mother.'

He picked his beer up and kicked Shitbag.

'Shit!' he exclaimed. 'Tell me what happened then?'

'You won't believe me anyway.'

'I will.'

'How old were you?' I asked.

'Twelve, sad to say,' he sighed.

'Cynthia?' I asked.

'Cynthia,' he confirmed.

We had known Cynthia since time began. Her family always got posted to the same place as us and she was one of those girls who believed it was her God-given duty to show all the little boys what to do with their little 'things'. Don't get me wrong, this is no criticism. We loved that girl to death; we worshipped the very ground she walked on; as far as we were concerned, she was a goddess.

'How many times since?' he asked.

'Do you mean times? Or with different girls? Because if you mean times then it's got to be at least one hundred on account of Cynthia.'

'Let's forget Cynthia. I mean different girls, not counting Cynthia, and we'd better not count Judith either.'

'I've never been near Judith!' I protested.

'Well you must be the only male object spread over four continents that hasn't!'

'Are we counting the three Potter sisters?' I asked.

'Christ!' he exclaimed. 'I'd forgotten all about them!'

'And what about New Zealanders?' I asked.

We had a large contingent of New Zealand girls at school and they were rather forward little creatures. In fact, not to put too fine a point on it, they went like hell.

'Oh God!' he swore. 'All right, no New Zealanders and forget the Potter sisters as well.'

I counted on my fingers.

'Seven. And you?'

He sighed again. 'Only five.'

We raised our beer cans to the prone figure in the chair.

'Cheers, mother!' we both called.

So, thanks to mother's lucid explanation of the facts of life we went armed into the big bad world with a considerable amount of knowledge that we felt sure most other teenagers lacked. But that whole business didn't mean much to me at the time because, as I was explaining, I'd taken to spending my time alone with the dogs. For about half a year after the big party and small riot, I did nothing more than fishing or exploring. The days passed and I suppose I turned into something of a lotus eater.

I had a small canoe, a present from Richard Chan. I kept it on the beach, which was just a short walk down the hill from our house, and most days I would throw the dogs on board and paddle over to the nearest island, Blakamati, the Island of the Dead. It earned this sinister name when five hundred bodies were unearthed on the main beach, where they had been buried by the Japanese during the war. Sometimes we would see sharks in the centre of the channel and the dogs would bark like hell at them. I used to swim across before I had the canoe, but then a girl I knew got eaten by a shark and I gave that up. One time I saw what could only have been a salt-water crocodile, a monster that dwarfed my canoe. I shut the dogs up when they started to bark at that one. The last thing I wanted was for that huge creature to take any notice of us.

On Blakamati there was a troop of crab-eating macaques which we had been having a running war with for over a year. They would watch us arrive and then come storming down to the beach to shout at us. The big males were brave and aggressive when they faced up to the dogs. They always had one hell of a noisy fight without actually making contact with one another; they just ran around in screaming circles with fangs bared. When things looked like they were getting out of hand I used to lob a few well-placed stones into the mêlée and break them up. Dogs and monkeys hate stones, and are suspicious of the magical way humans have of being able to cause hurt from fifty yards away.

Once we'd dispersed the macaques we would explore the endless mangrove swamps and tiny salt-water streams that cut deep into the island, completely covered by the spreading foliage of the mangroves so that they were like narrow green tunnels. The dogs would sit in the prow of the canoe, while I pushed them through the shallow, muddy, sea-snake infested water. Bright blue crabs crouched on the muddy banks and waved their single outsized claws at us in invitation; we always waved back. White egrets burst out of their hiding places to fly away on heavy beating wings. Sometimes we found really giant iguanas sleeping in the water. I never understood their behaviour. The iguanas would find a shallow spot and just lay under water, as if they were in a trance. You could pick them up by the tail and there would be no reaction at all.

Sometimes the macaques followed us, and when we came around a bend in the small stream they would be there, jumping up and down on the banks like demented pygmies, rolling their red eyes and swearing at us in monkey talk.

It was one of these monkeys that got me into very serious trouble and broke up my perfect little world: a monkey, and Jane, the ex-convent girl from the party with the troublesome piece of flesh. I thought I had seen the last of her and, as I said, I was in an anti-girl phase anyway, and had been pure for almost a year.

I was tying my canoe up to a tree on the island once, after a long day of fighting mad monkeys, when Jane suddenly appeared from behind the tree and said, 'Hi, dingbat, how's it going?'

'Christ!' I said.

'Is that it?' she asked. 'No passionate kiss or anything like that?'

'Christ!'

'Well, I thought you'd be glad to see me, at least!' she said, hands on hips. 'I've been waiting all bloody day for you to come back.'

'What the hell do you want, Jane?' I asked her.

'I come all the way over here and all you do is moan. I came to see you, as a matter of fact.'

'Who told you where I was.'

'Brother Dave,' she answered.

I made a mental note to break his legs, burn his new Van Morrison album and throw Shitbag at him when he was asleep at three in the morning.

She looked me over. She touched the scars on my arms where the dog had attacked me.

'What are those?' she asked.

'Dog bites.'

She touched the welts on my stomach.

'What are those?'

'Rabies injections.'

She started laughing. I didn't find it funny. I was proud of my scars.

'Are you really not pleased to see me?' she asked, coming

right up to me so I could feel the warmth from her body. She had a tiny bikini on, nothing else. I backed off.

'It's OK,' I said.

'Shall I say something dirty?' she asked.

'Well . . . ' I hesitated.

'What's wrong with you?' she demanded.

'Richard says girls are not good for my health,' I explained.

'*Richard*!' she screamed. 'Who the fuck is Richard for Christ's sake?'

'He's a friend of mine.'

'Well he doesn't know fuck all!'

'Actually he knows quite a lot . . . '

'You dingbat!' she yelled. 'Don't you realise that there are about twenty guys who want to go out with me?'

'Well, go out with them then!' I shouted back.

'I don't want to! God help me, but I want to go out with you!'

'Oh,' I said.

She stormed off up the beach, collected her things and marched up the steps. But she was back the next day.

And I'd thought a lot about her, and her warm body in the tiny bikini, during the night and had come to the conclusion that just one girl wouldn't be that bad for my health. So when I saw her sunbathing I went over and said 'Hi.' We had a long chat about everything except what we really wanted to talk about until she asked me about the Island of the Dead and what I did over there.

'Just exploring and playing with the monkeys,' I told her.

'What is there to explore?' she asked.

I told her about the hidden Japanese bunker I had found, complete with the skeletal remains of soldiers and old rusted-away rifles.

'Will you show it to me?' she asked.

'It's my own secret place. I don't want to show it to other people really,' I answered.

'If you show me, I'll give you something very special.'

'Like what?'

'I'm still a virgin you know,' she announced.

'Christ!' I said.

'If you take me over, now, you can do it to me in the bunker. You can deflower me right there, against a dirty wall or something.'

'Christ, Jane, you shouldn't talk like that.'

'Why not? You like it really, you little bastard. Well? Are we going or not?'

I nodded my head.

'But if I let you do it to me, you've got to promise something else,' she warned.

'What, Jane?'

'That you'll go out with me, properly – promise!'

'I swear on my mother's bedsocks.'

'That'll do,' she said. 'Let's go and be naughty!'

She tried to make me leave the dogs behind but I told her there was no way I was setting foot on that island inhabited by a crazy gang of macaques without my hounds to protect me. Half way across in the canoe she really shocked me by asking casually, 'How would you like to see my breasts?'

Then she pulled her bikini top down to her waist. I'd never really seen a girl's breasts before. OK, I had done it with a few girls, but I generally closed my eyes and did it either in the dark or under a blanket by Braille. And none of the girls was built like Jane. I had seen Mrs James in the bath, but this was something altogether different.

I was frightened and fascinated. Her nipples were dark brown and bigger than my fists, and there was something about the way her breasts hung that just tore my stomach apart.

'What do you think?' she asked.

'Jesus!' I replied.

'Is that all? Do you like them?'

'Jesus, yes!'

'What do you think about my nipples?'

'Jesus!'

She slapped them about a bit.

'I think my breasts are my best feature, don't you?'

As she said this she brought them together, making her cleavage immense.

I hadn't moved the paddle for the whole time and the canoe was drifting out to sea.

'Christ, Jane! Put them away. I can't paddle while you've got them out.'

She slipped her bikini top back up.

'I just thought you'd like a preview of what you're going to get in a minute,' she said.

I started to paddle again.

'Shall I say something dirty?' she asked.

'Just shut up until we get there, please?'

We drew up to the beach, and the first thing I saw was a Malay fisherman beating a very large male macaque over the head with a heavy wooden club. The monkey was chained to a tree and couldn't get away, but it was still putting up one hell of a fight, trying to get a hold on the man so it could bite him. Every time the man got in a good blow on the monkey's head he shouted out in English, 'Now you die bastard!' Whack!

They were about a hundred yards up the beach so I sent the dogs to interview them until I could get there. They got stuck straight in there, forcing the man to leave the monkey alone while he tried to keep the dogs off his legs. I ran up the beach and called them off and asked him what was going on.

He told me that he had had the macaque since it was a baby, ten years ago, and it had been the family pet; but now it was older it had turned vicious and kept on attacking his wife and kids. He couldn't think of any other way of getting rid of it apart from beating it to death. He had released it twice but each time it came back to the house and bit someone.

While we were discussing the story I watched the macaque and he didn't seem so bad. Only when one of the dogs came a bit close did he bare his wicked fangs in warning. Most of the time he was rubbing his obviously sore head.

Jane was still sat in the canoe watching all this in some amazement. The man told me I could have the beast on condition that I remove it from his island. We shook hands on the deal and I undid the monkey's chain and led him down to the canoe with the dogs bringing up the rear. The look on both the dogs' faces implied that they had just captured their first prisoner.

'What the hell are you doing with that animal?' Jane demanded.

'Taking it home.'

'How?'

'In the canoe, of course.'

'Not with me in it!'

'I can't leave the monkey here. The man will kill it.'

'I don't give a damn. I don't want that monkey in this boat, it will attack me.'

'Well you stay here then, and I'll come back for you later.'

She looked at the Malay fisherman, who was watching us with a big grin on his face. It was a very lonely beach, miles from the nearest village.

'I'm not staying on the beach with that Malay!'

'Don't worry, I won't let the monkey hurt you . . . you can sit behind me and the dogs . . . you'll be safe.'

'I thought you and me were going to look at the bunker and do it there. Don't you want to do it to me?'

This was blackmail.

'Jane. This monkey comes back with me in the canoe, now. Whether you come or not is up to you.'

She started crying.

'What do you want a smelly old monkey for anyway?' she asked through her tears.

'I am going to train it to be a bodyguard. Can you imagine that. A fully grown macaque with the dogs. Unbeatable!'

She obviously did not share my excitement about the monkey. I forced her out of the canoe and secured the monkey tightly to the prow by his chain. I told the dogs to sit in front of me and then loaded the weeping Jane behind me. We set out for home. It was a very crowded little canoe.

It was OK to start with, but then the macaque realised he was out on the open water and went berserk. I don't mean normal berserk: I mean this animal went over the rails in a big way. He started leaping and shrieking and tearing at his chain, and in his fury he managed to loosen it. The dogs had had enough of this unruly behaviour and set about the miscreant in no mean fashion. The canoe was rocking about like crazy. Jane was screaming from her perch right at the back of the canoe, almost in the water. The dogs ended up in the prow with bared teeth and bitten bums while the monkey tried to sit on my lap. I had to hit it with the paddle to keep it off. By now we were shipping water at an alarming rate. One stroke in the water and then one on the monkey's head. It was painfully slow progress for a long time.

The minute the canoe touched the beach the monkey sat down calmly and rubbed his head. Jane, who had spent the entire journey with most of her body outside the canoe, jumped out and stood on the beach with her hands on her hips, looking at me. It was not a friendly look.

'Shit!' she screamed. 'Shit! You bastard! I offer you my virginity and you take a monkey instead. That's it! I mean that is bloody it. I'd rather do it with a dog. Stuff you and stuff your bloody monkey!'

Then she was gone, storming up the beach under a black cloud. Well, I thought. That is very definitely the end of that little romance.

The monkey was very calm in comparison with Jane and simply followed me up the hill towards the house. I didn't have to pull on the chain or anything. He tagged along like a corgi. I tied him to the big breadfruit tree so that his chain allowed him to go right to the top as well as the freedom to wander about twenty feet away from the tree. The dogs sat in the shade and watched him, still acting as if he was their prisoner. I fixed him a bowl of water and some fruit and went to lay down for a while. I was exhausted, and very sulky about not doing it with Jane in the bunker.

Sometime later I heard my mother shouting from outside, so I went to see what was going on.

'There is an animal in the tree!' she said, pointing at the macaque, who was half way up.

'It's a monkey,' I told her calmly.

'A monkey?'

'A crab-eating macaque. He is very friendly.'

'But I don't want a crab-eating macaque in my garden. The smell will be awful.'

'What smell?' I asked.

'From the dead crabs, of course!'

'What dead crabs, mother?'

'From the crabs it eats. I don't suppose for one minute it will eat the shells as well.'

'No, no, mother. That's just a name. He eats fruits and stuff like that, same as any other monkey.'

'Are you sure it is friendly?'

'Of course, he wouldn't hurt a fly, mother.'

'Well, I suppose it can stay for a while then. But you will have to do something with it before your father comes home.'

She went to go, but then stopped again.

'Who was that girl?' she asked.

'What girl?'

'The girl who was here earlier, crying and asking to use the telephone?'

'Oh, *that* girl you mean. I don't know. She was on the beach. What did you say to her?'

'I told her we didn't have a telephone.'

'What did she say then?'

'That was the funny part. She was quite rude. She said, "No, families of savages often don't." I really didn't know what the girl was talking about. A pretty young thing, too.'

'Yes, mother,' I said and she wandered off somewhere in her usual vague fashion.

I think given more time I would have been able to turn that monkey into a friendly individual, but as usual events moved on ahead of me and all my careful plans got left behind. I never meant to do these things to my father. It just happened like that.

He was supposed to be away for another month at least, but his ship got badly damaged during an encounter with an Indonesian gunboat and they had to limp back to Singapore for repairs. He came through the garden gate in a state of extreme exhaustion and was attacked by the monkey. There is something about men in uniforms that brings the worst out in any animal. That monkey really laid into him. We were sat reading in the living room when we heard the bellowing of my father, quickly followed by the mad chattering of a male macaque on the attack. These noises were soon joined by the baying of the dogs as they joined in the fray. We rushed outside to see my father fending the furious beast off with his leather briefcase while the dogs ran around snapping at them both.

'Dear God!' exclaimed mother with some feeling.

'What the bloody hell is this?' father roared, also with some feeling.

Before I had a chance to intervene, the macaque tore his chain out of the tree, bit my father very neatly on the arm and ran off down the road, dragging his chain behind him.

My mother whispered, 'I should disappear if I were you.'

You couldn't see my dust. I hid in the nearby jungle and watched my mother leading my poor father into the house. Using stealth and cover I worked my way back through the garden until I was hidden under the window and could hear their conversation. Mother was making soothing noises. My father wasn't hysterical but I could tell he was close to breaking point. It was the longest speech I ever heard my father make.

'I can't believe this family. I go away for two months, my ship is blown away from under me by communists, my crew sneaks up the tower of the main mosque in Brunei and substitute the call-to-prayer record with the Beatles' "Twist and Shout". There is a full-scale riot when that blares out at six in the morning. Some CIA agent chucks a grenade into the toilet-ditch for a joke when I'm taking a crap and blows me across the clearing covered in shit, then I come home and am attacked by a bloody baboon on my own doorstep. Jesus H. Christ! This is really too much. I am going to get drunk and forget about everything. What a family! Last time I came home there wasn't a beer can left in the fridge and every single one of my sons was wandering about the house as pissed as a newt. I needn't remind you that the youngest boy is only seven years old! When I went to shout at Dave about it he was in bed with some girl, both of them stark naked and drunk. The time before that the bastards wrecked all the furniture and destroyed the house with that party. I still haven't lived that down! As for that other one, the one with foot and mouth disease, I no longer consider that boy my son. If I see him I will very likely strangle him. You don't have to tell me it was him who brought that bloody oversized baboon into my house, I know it. I know it only too bloody well. I cannot take any more of this. I will move into the officers' mess until this posting is over. At least there I can sit and have a drink without being attacked by baboons, disturbed by the multiple reports of my sons' deaths, injuries sustained in riots and gang wars with Triads, and diseases – rabies for Christ's sake – without having people wreck my career, my house and my . . . Shit! I have had enough of the lot of you. I need a beer!'

I heard him walk into the kitchen and open the heavy fridge door. There was a sudden explosive screech followed by a bellow of rage and a loud crash. Shitbag came hurtling around the corner of the house, hissing like a small steam train and with all his hair stood on end, crashed into me, then disappeared in the direction of the jungle.

'Shit!' my father screamed. 'The bloody cat was in the fridge again. The bastard attacked me. Christ! I think I need stitches!'

Things went from bad to worse. I hid in the kampong. The monkey went on the rampage and the army were called out to shoot him. Just before they got him with a bullet he decided to attack the daughter of my father's commanding officer and bit her very savagely on her left breast. That was a very long, hard nail in my coffin – my father actually came down to the kampong looking for me. He had murder in his eyes, Richard assured me. After that we communicated only by hand-carried messages.

And I thought a lot about Jane and her amazing breasts, and promised myself that if – and it was a very big if – Jane gave me another shot at her virginity I would not mess it up. I should have left that monkey right on the beach with that fisherman whacking it around the head screaming, 'Now you die bastard!' Whack!

9

This going back into the past is damned good for my nerves – they have flattened out a bit and I'm down to one bottle of gin per day. OK, still with about twenty cans of Tiger, but believe me it's better than it was. I haven't even thought about that bastard the Boss, or Thailand, and I started this whole thing off to write about them. Stuff the Boss. For the first time in eight years I actually feel quite normal, something that might pass for a human rather than the half-crazed, spittle-flecked baboon that's been sitting on my shoulder all this time directing operations in the brothel.

My father was spitting blood after the monkey attacked him. It was my fault, but I didn't purposefully set out to do it. My mother could see that but he couldn't. So I lived in the kampong with Richard for a long time. I didn't mind. We did a lot of cock-fighting and fishing and it was always great to be around Richard. He thought it was funny that my father wanted me dead. He'd wrap his gigantic arms around me and say, 'You're a guy! I love you so much I could break all the bones in your body!'

We only disagreed on one point: girls. He was really fanatical about how bad they were for your health. It was his favourite subject. In his world even self-abuse was bad. He used to lay back in his hammock, a whisky glass in his hand

and a gigantic cigar in his mouth, and lecture me on the evils of copulation and masturbation.

One evening I'd had enough and astonished him by interrupting him and saying 'I reckon smoking and drinking whisky is a lot worse than screwing.'

He spat his cigar out, threw his whisky glass on the ground and leaped out of his hammock.

'Watch this!' he commanded, and crouched down low on his haunches in front of the wooden wall of his house. Uttering a terrifying bellow he launched himself at the wall and with a blurring round of savage kicks and punches smashed his way straight through. He just disintegrated that wall. Shattered planks and boards flew into the air, and one of them whacked me right in the head and it hurt like hell. After no more than three seconds, Richard was stood grinning at me beside the wreckage of his house. Behind him, his bemused parents sat at the table where they had been enjoying a cup of tea.

'See?' he asked.

I nodded my head in agreement.

'That's all the time I need. Two seconds, maybe three. I didn't even breathe once. It don't matter a damn how much I smoke or drink, it ain't ever going to affect those two seconds. OK?' he asked.

'OK,' I agreed.

He laid back in his hammock with a new cigar and a new whisky. 'Now, as for women . . . ' he started on.

If Richard had to go six rounds with Mohammed Ali he would have been exhausted, but the point was he would never have gone six rounds with Mohammed Ali. No, Richard would have creamed him in the first three seconds. I'd never seen anybody who could cram so much animal energy and power into such a small amount of time.

Chinese New Year was not far away when my brother Dave made a surprise visit. He was drunk and we were playing mah-jong in an eating house when he staggered in.

'God bless Mr Lee Kuan Facking Yew!' he shouted after colliding with several walls and finally ending up at our table.

'Don't I know you?' he asked, staring at me. 'Aren't you the little bastard that substituted my dearest mother's contraceptives for indigestion pills and caused the unwanted arrival of those two little buggers I am forced to call brothers?'

'Yes, that's me all right,' I assured him.

He shook my hand.

'Good man! Good man! Waiter! A case of Tiger beer here, on my father's account.'

'What do you want, you mad bastard?' I asked once he was settled and nursing his Tiger. There was always something totally irresistible about Dave when he was drunk. His black eyes shone and you just loved him to death.

Richard laid four beautiful dragon stones down, much to the dismay of the other two players, and looked at us.

'You guys!' he said, and laughed.

'I have two messages for you, both of extreme importance to your embittered and pointless life,' Dave announced. 'The first is that you are to be allowed back in the family fold for Chinese New Year. We are invited to Ma Lee's house tomorrow and mother has decided to permit you to join us. Needless to say father will not be there.'

Ma Lee was our long-suffering amah and an invitation to her house was not to be missed. She was the best cook in the whole damned world.

'And the other message?' I asked.

'Aha! You are going to love this one, blood relation of mine. You are invited to a party in Singapore next week.'

'I don't go to parties in Singapore, you know that.'

He wagged a finger in front of my nose. 'Oh, but I think you'll go to this one. A certain young lady has specifically requested your attendance at her sixteenth birthday party.'

'What certain young lady is that?'

'A certain ex-convent type of young lady who seems determined to give you what she will not give to anyone else.'

'Not Jane!'

'The one and same . . . coming? I mean, it's not everyone

who has a party to give away their virginity. Once you've got it you can pin it up on the wall and we can throw darts at it!'

'I wouldn't miss it for the world,' I assured him, and he staggered out with a final, 'God bless Mr Lee Kuan Facking Yew!' and with Rape and Pillage wagging their tails behind him. We sort of shared the dogs in those days.

Jane! Dear God, this time there was going to be no mistake. But first there was Chinese New Year at Ma Lee's – I was determined to make no mistakes there either. I had to score plenty of Brownie points with mother so she would convince father that I had a better side. It was there somewhere, you just had to look pretty deep.

Ma Lee lived on the far edge of the kampong in a tiny house built up on stilts standing out over the water. It was a well-kept, clean house with the usual horde of children and the inevitable Chinese husband dressed in the standard uniform of all Chinese husbands: baggy shorts and white T-shirt with a large hole in one armpit and another just below the right breast. Chinese husbands are always the same. They never work but sit in dark corners of the house drinking huge quantities of whisky and smiling at visitors with their gold teeth.

Ma Lee's cooking was a dream: exotic *maa-mee*, hot chilli noodles with fresh squid, prawns, crab, octopus, oysters and grouper. Mother loved it. Father hated it, but he wasn't there. We all sat at the table eating, when Dave decided to make the introductions. 'Mother, you might remember this horrible example of a boy from somewhere. Underneath that long hair and dirt is none other than your second-born child.'

Ma Lee asked what we wanted to drink.

'Gin,' said mother.

'Beer,' said Dave. Mother's eyes narrowed slightly.

'Beer,' I said. Mother's eyes glinted.

'Beer please!' shouted the two small brothers.

'Oh no!' Mother said. 'No beer for you two. You'll have to drink something else.'

They looked at each other and shrugged their shoulders. 'Gin?' they ventured.

'You can give them lemonade, Ma Lee,' mother said firmly.

I smiled into every corner of the room and was rewarded in the last corner by the glint of gold teeth. Dave showed his own gold teeth off towards the same corner and the returning flash was even brighter.

'Husband,' Ma Lee explained when she brought the drinks. 'He no speak English.'

He came out of the corner, grinning and bowing. He shook mother's hand.

'Whisky!' he declared.

Then he moved round the table and shook us all by the hand calling out 'Whisky!' each time. When it was my turn I stood up and said to him, 'Whisky!'

His grin nearly split his face and he pumped my hand up and down. 'Whisky!' he shouted.

'Whisky!' I shouted back.

He went off into his corner, and came back with a bottle of whisky. He held it up and called out in triumph, 'Whisky!'

'Whisky!' we all called out, with the exception of mother who stared sternly at Dave and me. The husband set seven glass tumblers on the table and filled them up to the brim. Mother stared about in helpless horror. Dave and I held our glasses up.

'Cheers!' we called out.

'Whisky!' the husband replied, and we downed the lot.

The little brothers tried to follow suit but mother slapped their hands away from the glasses.

'Come on, mother,' Dave urged. 'It's all part of the Chinese New Year celebrations.'

'He will be horribly upset if you refuse to drink it,' I added.

With a grimace she sipped at her whisky. Ma Lee had been continually loading mother's drink – I reckoned one of her gins would have been enough to cripple a Waterloo wino – and mother was beginning to look a trifle confused. She failed to notice the small brothers sneaking their tumblers full of whisky off the table and sipping them out of view. They were both smirking like mad and hiccuping. Every time either Dave's or my glass was empty the beaming husband filled it up again saying, 'Whisky!'

Mother, trying hard to be polite, engaged Ma Lee in a confusing conversation which I don't believe either understood a single word of. The small brothers were by now under the table, giggling to themselves and knocking their heads noisily on the underside. Dave stood up unsteadily from the table, veered suddenly across the room, and collided with the flimsy wall, dislodging a picture of some Chinese saint. He carefully put the picture back up, upside down, and then asked Ma Lee for the toilet. She spoke to her husband in Chinese and he led Dave away, grinning and holding onto his arm. He returned a few seconds later, filled up the glasses, and sat down at the table with us. Mother stared at him with a fearsome expression.

'Who is that Chinese man?' she demanded with a considerable slur.

'That's Ma Lee's husband, mother,' I said.

'But what's he doing sitting at our dining table?' she asked.

I patted her on the arm.

'We are at Ma Lee's house, mother. This is Ma Lee's table.'

She looked about with a dazed expression. 'Well, in that case I suppose it's all right then,' she said.

Further meaningless conversation was interrupted by a splintering crash from somewhere at the back of the house, followed quickly by the sound of manic laughter. We all – apart from the little brothers who were still under the table – rushed to the back of the house to investigate. A small corridor led outside onto the boardwalks that connected all the houses. The toilet was out there somewhere, but it was as black as pitch and we couldn't see a thing until Ma Lee's husband brought a storm lantern. Then we could make out that one side of the flimsy toilet, built over the sea, had collapsed. It was hanging down over the side and you could see right into the primitive toilet, which was no more than a hole in the floor. In the darkness below us someone started laughing like a crazy loon. Ma Lee's husband hung the lantern over the side of the boardwalk and we saw Dave, laid on his back in the mud and shit and laughing his head off. He had obviously staggered into the toilet and fallen straight out of the side.

Ma Lee gazed down at him in horror.

'Very sorry, miss,' she said to mother.

Her husband grinned and waved with his free hand.

'Whisky!' he shouted.

'You drunken bastard,' I shouted.

Dave shouted back, waving his arms.

'I'm in the shit again!'

Mother shouted out to him, 'Come out of there at once, you are making a fool of me.'

'Whisky!' shouted the husband again.

It was not possible to get Dave out of the mud and shit there so he had to wade through about two hundred yards of it to reach the shore. Back indoors the little brothers were still chortling away underneath the table, and I noticed that all our whisky glasses had been emptied. We all sat down and the husband refilled the glasses. Dave walked in the door looking like a mud monster and stinking very strongly of shit. He sat down with a sigh, picked up his glass and threw the whisky down in one go.

'Someone shat on my head,' he said, sadly.

'Here's to Jane,' I said, and stood up.

Dave stood up.

'Here's to Judith,' he said.

'The Potter sisters,' I offered.

'Mother, stand up,' Dave ordered. 'We are making toasts.'

She climbed unsteadily to her feet and held her gin up.

'To all the girls from down-under,' I said.

'Which is exactly where they all belong,' said Dave. 'Cheers!'

The husband called out, 'Whisky!', and mother poured her gin straight down her cleavage. She looked very annoyed when she found there was nothing left in her glass.

Suddenly there was a frantic barking from outside, quickly followed by a series of sharp bangs. A small brown kampong dog came hurtling in through the doorway with a string of exploding firecrackers tied to its tail. There must have been two hundred of the powerful fireworks blazing away there. The animal had blind terror in its eyes and was trying as fast as it could to get away from the crackers, which of course it couldn't. It sprinted around and around the room accompanied by a volley of explosions, setting fire to some drapes in one corner, and then disappeared lickety-split under the table. The small brothers came hurtling out of the other side, in wild panic but still clutching their whisky glasses, and threw themselves into a corner with their arms over their heads. God only knows what they thought was going on – it must have sounded like the Indonesian Army had invaded their drinking den. There was another resounding salvo of reports, the table shook, glasses and dishes crashed to the floor, and the room was filled with clouds of drifting black smoke. Finally the dog emerged from under the table at a million miles an hour and shot out of the door.

Ma Lee's husband stood up and pointed in the general direction of the departed exploding dog.

'Whisky,' he said.

'Whisky,' Dave and I agreed.

Mother picked herself up from the floor where she had thrown herself upon the arrival of the exploding dog.

'Just once, just once,' she said, 'I would like to have a normal evening out with my family.'

She shook her head, slowly and sadly, and walked out of the door.

Richard poked his head through the door, took in the sight of Dave slumped in his chair covered in shit, the small brothers weeping and trembling in the corner, Ma Lee wailing and pulling her hair out, me and the husband standing up and toasting each other in a room full of smoke with broken glasses and dishes littering the floor.

'You guys!' he said, and came in and had a whisky.

Jane. I even had a shower and washed my hair for the first time in months. This was going to be the big one. The thought of her warm body had been making me shiver for at least a week.

The evening started off well enough. Richard came over to the mainland with me and we hit a few bars and watched a few cock-fights along the Bukit Timah road; then Richard went off to the New Stadium to watch Thai boxing and I took a Changi bus to the British Military Hospital, where the party was being held. Jane's father, who was a surgeon or something, was away on holiday and had left Jane to look after the place.

The BMH was huge. I couldn't find the damned house and ended up in a Chinese bar drinking Tiger till my small amount of money was gone. Then I found the Officers' Mess and was refused a drink; when I tried to put it on my father's bill I was promptly shown the door. I somehow landed up next outside the NCOs' Mess where there was a hell of a party going on in the garden, rock band and everything. I got absolutely bombed on Tiger with a bunch of Malay NCOs, and we ended up smoking grass together. Then I discovered they were the band and they started saying I was the drummer, so we fell about the stage trying to play 'She Loves You'. We had to stop when some of the other NCOs got rowdy and threw beer cans at us. Two of the band members drove me to the other side of the hospital grounds and let me out of the car in what looked like the middle of nowhere. My head hurt and my world was spinning around at a hundred miles an hour so I sat on the kerb and concentrated on the ground. A silver Austin Healey 3000 convertible arrived and the driver, who came complete with leather flying-hat and goggles, said, 'Hi, I'm Ashley. Can I give you a lift somewhere?'

I thought I was probably hallucinating but got in the car anyway. He drove at incredible speed on the narrow roads of the BMH, round and round in circles. This did not help my head.

'Where are you going?' he shouted out above the din of the howling motor.

'To a party!' I shouted back.

'Where?' he shouted.

'Don't know!' I shouted back.

He slammed the brakes on making the car slew across the road.

'I reckon this must be it,' he said, leaning over and unlocking the door for me. I got out and said, 'Thanks.'

He waved his hand and skidded the car down the road. Jesus, I thought. Was that for real or what?

Before me was a bungalow with fairy lights strung up in the trees, a subdued beat coming out of its open shutters and people moving about in the garden.

I stood unsteadily, the house falling in and out of my vision, and felt as happy as I had ever been – apart from the pain in my head . . . It was all just so damned perfect: the white bungalow with its coloured lights drifting in the cool breeze and the soft music coming out of the grounds. Then I realised I needed to piss very urgently, and also the idea of vomiting flew up from my stomach and started flapping round my head, beating me with its wings. I staggered into the garden, stumbling past people who were holding drinks until I knocked into them, and walked straight into a swimming pool without changing stride.

The water exploded around me and then I was enveloped in a bubble of stillness and silence. I drifted down very slowly, leaving a flowing trail of silver bubbles that ran out of my clothes and pearled upwards to break the surface of the pool, still rippling from the impact of my body. I touched the bottom without feeling it and sat down in a lotus position, then looked up at the surface. It was a sea of glimmering mercury, and if I let a small bubble of air out it wobbled upwards until it burst on the silvery surface. It was like being encased in a jewel. Twenty seconds must have passed. My lungs started to squeeze. Thirty seconds and the pain became acute and lazy black spots swam in front of my eyes. Under normal circumstances I could swim two complete lengths of a standard pool underwater, but this was not normal. There were at least fourteen cans of Tiger beer looking for a way out of my stomach and the smokes had given me severe brain damage. I was seriously thinking about dying for the pleasure of the silvery stillness and enormous silence that the pool was offering. Suddenly there was a dull thud and the entire perfect surface of the pool shattered, and a small black-haired angel grinned down at me, kicked her legs and was by my side. She tried to lift me by the arms, but I pushed her hands away, drove every bit of air out of me and kicked myself up to the surface in clouds of bubbles. As I shot out of the water I gulped in air before falling back under, then bobbed back to the surface. The girl came up to me and put a hand on my shoulder.

'Are you OK?' she asked. 'I thought you were dead.'

I went to say 'Yes', but instead fourteen cans of Tiger beer finally found their exit point and I ejected a stream of vomit into the pool. A man standing at the edge of the pool screamed at me, 'Get that filth out of my pool!'

The girl took my head and swam backwards with me to the edge. She put my hands on the side of the pool.

'Are you OK, now?' she asked.

I nodded my head, too frightened to try speech again – yet. The man was striding, in what looked like a grim fit, around the pool to where we were resting.

'That's my father,' she said, then asked, 'Who the hell are you, anyway?'

'I love you,' I told her, and it came out as words instead of liquid.

'My father won't love you. The pool is full of vomit and they were going to have a swim later.'

Her father arrived.

'What the hell do you think you are doing in my swimming pool? Get out of there! Filth! I hope you do not know this . . . this person, Maria?' he shouted.

I ducked my head under the water for ten, twenty seconds . . . Then I looked up and he was gone.

She jumped up on the side of the pool, sat down and put a hand out to me.

'You'd better get out and run away, fast. Father has just gone to call the Military Police. What were you doing in our pool anyway?'

I sat down by her and we dangled our legs in the water.

'I think I got the wrong party,' I explained.

'I think you did as well. This is my parent's silver wedding anniversary.'

'Oh God!' I groaned.

'Did you mean it? What you said just now?' she asked.

'Yes, Maria.'

'Oh.'

'Can you get away from here?' I asked her.

'Why?' she asked.

'I already told you.'

'Oh.'

She stared at the ripples her feet were making in the water.

'Yes, I would like that,' she said.

I touched her arm.

'I'll run away now, before your father gets back. I'll wait for you in the bushes across the road. OK?'

She nodded her head and I took off. She came twenty minutes later with her breath coming hard and fast and slid her arm through mine.

'Phew. I waited until his back was turned and then ran out.'

'Will you get into trouble?' I asked.

'Oh yes.'

She was thirteen. I was fifteen. She had pale skin for Singapore and startling green eyes. They looked like she had stolen them off some cat.

'But not as much trouble as you if the army cops get their hands on you,' she added.

'What did the cat say?' I asked her.

'What cat?' she asked back.

'The cat you stole those eyes from?'

She laughed. She had a great laugh.

We ducked down in the bushes. We both knew the special noise of army Landrover tyres, and could hear the Military Police one sweep past, heading for her house. She smiled at me.

'Nobody was ever sick in our pool before. It was ace!'

'I don't think your father thought so.'

'Oh, he's a stuffy old fart anyway,' she said. 'What are we going to do now?'

'Let's get lost in this jungle,' I suggested, and we pushed

our way through the dense, scratchy vegetation hand in hand. In a small clearing fringed with dark palms we stopped and looked at each other.

'How come you are so pale?' I asked her.

'I never go out in the sun, my skin burns very badly, and I'm flabby as well.'

She stood there in her wet white shorts and wet white blouse with about as much meat on her as a starved whippet.

'Flabby!' I laughed.

She held a leg up and slapped the thigh with her hand.

'Yeah, look at that leg, flabby.'

'Christ! Maria, you are the best looking thing I ever saw in my whole pitiful life, animal, vegetable or mineral.'

'I don't even know your name,' she said.

'I don't think introductions are necessary. After all I have been sick in your swimming pool.'

'I'd still like to know your name.'

I told her.

'Don't kiss me.' She warned as we laid down on the soft brown earth.

'Why not?' I asked.

'Because it's yukky,' she said with a giggle. 'I hate being kissed. Fathers and aunties kiss you. Yuk.'

'You aren't a virgin are you?'

She laughed and shook her head. 'Don't be silly!'

'Thank Christ for that!' I said, and we did it to each other until the big tiger ants ran over us and bit us and bit us and made us stop.

'Does that mean we are going out with each other?' she asked when we were brushing ants and debris off our damp clothes.

'I'd like that very much, Maria.'

'So would I.'

So we shook hands, on account of kissing being 'yukky'.

'What about this party?' she asked.

'Oh.'

'Are you still going?' she persisted. 'I'm just in the mood for a party. It's too early to go home and be murdered by my father.'

I thought, What the hell! And grabbed her hand. 'Let's go.'

She knew the grounds of the BMH better than me and had a good idea where the party should be. We stopped one time on the way – we just had to do it again, quickly, standing up. When we got to the party, the place was heaving with people dancing to a live band, shouting and drinking, even though it was late. You know how it is when you arrive at a party where everybody knows you but nobody knows the girl you are with? That's how it was: everyone staring at Maria and wondering who the hell she was, and why we both looked like drowned rats. I was worrying about one thing only: Jane, and her reaction to Maria. I was hoping it was so late that she was either bombed out of her brains or with someone else. We stayed in the garden, drinking cold Tiger from a big wooden tub full of ice. I asked after Dave.

'Over there,' someone said, waving vaguely towards the back garden.

We found him asleep in a big monsoon drain, an empty bottle of aspirins clutched in his hand. A girl was stretched out like a broken puppet by his side, her dress up around her waist, knickers missing and a big spider sitting on her nose. Scattered around them were about twenty beer cans.

'Are they friends of yours?' Maria asked.

I pointed at Dave. 'That miserable object there is my brother. The girl I don't know, but I would say she is a New Zealander.'

'Why do you think she is from New Zealand?' Maria asked.

'Because she has her dress up over her waist.'

'I'm not a New Zealander and I had my shorts around my ankles a few minutes ago,' she insisted.

'I'm not going to argue with you. When she comes out of her coma we'll talk to her. I know I'm right.'

I poured the remains of my ice-cold beer over Dave's head. He spluttered, shook his head, and blinked up at us.

'Christ! If it isn't my dearest brother.'

'What's with the aspirins?' I asked.

'Suicide,' he replied, rubbing his head.

'Why suicide?' I asked.

'Well, I got drunk, I had sex, got drunk again, had sex again and thought to myself what do I do now and came up with suicide.' He looked at the girl in the ditch next to him. 'Who the hell is that?' he asked.

'I think she's a New Zealander,' I said.

'Your powers of observation amaze me. Christ, I could kill a great aunt for an ice-cold beer. My mouth is like the bottom of a parrot's cage.'

He pulled himself out of the gutter and noticed Maria for the first time.

'Who the hell is that?' he asked.

'Maria . . . we are . . . emmm . . . going out with one another,' I said.

'Well good luck to the pair of you,' he said. 'I'm sure Jane will be over the moon to meet your new girlfriend.'

And off he went to get a beer.

'Who's Jane?' Maria asked.

'Just an old friend.'

I was still hoping that Jane would be otherwise occupied. We went into the house where a band was playing in a big room with all the shutters thrown open to the night sky. We danced for a bit while the band played *Midnight Hour* and then we got a drink. Maria had a whisky, and I found an ice-cold beer right at the bottom of a big tub full of water.

Suddenly Jane burst through the door in a very drunken condition. She saw us and staggered over, spilled an entire glass of something very cold down the front of my trousers, threw her glass at the wall behind us, then slapped Maria around the face. 'Bitch!' she snarled, and fell away into the dancers.

Maria held up a hand to her burning cheek.

'Is that your old friend?' she asked.

'Yes, I think she was expecting something from me tonight,' I answered.

'Something like "doing" you mean?' she asked.

'Yes. She's still a virgin and I was supposed to relieve her of that terrible burden.'

She put her arm round my shoulders.

'Well, she's going to be disappointed then, and if the cow comes within spitting distance I'll knock her frikking teeth out of her ugly head.'

'Come on,' I said, and we went to find a quiet spot in the garden where there were no tiger ants. Directly we were away from the noise of the band we could hear what sounded like a Siberian tiger being violently ill. The noise was coming from the darkness of a giant palm tree. When we got close enough we could see it was a couple furiously copulating, him grunting and her roaring. I dragged the reluctant Maria over and we stood right above them, watching. It was the girl from the gutter and if she had had her eyes open she would have seen us. He had the back of his head to us, but I recognised the back of that head: it was Mr bloody Perfect, the underpant's advert. Oh boy, was I happy to see that jerk. I slapped his white arse as hard as I could. He stopped grunting and swung his head up to look at me.

'What the hell . . . ' he shouted. And then his words fell back down his throat when he recognised me. She stared up at us with nothing but annoyance on her face.

'Piss off, will ya!' she shouted in a strongly accented voice.

Maria was laughing.

'I am sorry to bother you at such an indelicate moment, but could you tell us whether you come from New Zealand?' I asked.

'Shaa-it!' she screamed. 'I'm from bloody Wellington, all right?'

'Thank you,' I said and we walked on.

'Told you so,' I said to a laughing Maria.

'I hope your bum isn't as white and spotty as that!' she said.

'Never looked,' I answered.

The couple's shouted conversation drifted over to us.

'I can't any more,' he said.

'Get on with it!' she demanded.

'He put me off.'

'Shaa-it!' she screamed, and then we lost them. And then we found our own palm.

Dave found us much later. He had a couple of ice-cold beers and he gave me one.

'Do you,' he asked Maria, 'have a father who is generally distinguished by smoke coming out of his nostrils and a rocket up his arse?'

'That sounds like him, why?' she asked.

'He was just here with a couple of uniformed heavies looking for you, and our friend Jane told him that the two of you were here together just a few minutes before he arrived.'

'Oh God,' I groaned.

'My father is the Commanding Officer here and he is a gold-plated bastard,' Maria assured us.

'Good luck,' Dave said, tossing me his spare bottle of aspirins, and setting off into the jungle in the opposite direction to the party. I didn't see him again for many months.

'I'm not going home,' Maria assured me.

I didn't blame her. When her father saw the state of her he would probably horse-whip her and make her have tests to see if her virginity was intact, and when it wasn't then I would be sitting in the shit up to my neck, as usual. We sat for a long time, drinking and deciding what to do. Finally we went back to the party, while no doubt the Military Police combed the grounds of the BMH looking for Maria.

There was hardly anybody left. The band and nearly everyone else had cleared out soon after the arrival of the Military Police. Sat at a large round table playing some sort of game were Jane, who looked a lot more sober than earlier, two other girls I didn't know, and one other girl I knew very well, the infamous Judith.

'Why did you tell her father that she was here and with me?' I asked Jane.

'Why not?' she replied.

'Because you just got me into very serious shit, that's why not you silly cow!'

'It's where you belong, honey,' she said with a sweet smile. The three other girls agreed with smiles of their own.

I found some semi-cold beers and gave Maria one. She wasn't worried about anything except having a good time.

For a thirteen-year-old, she had a very cool and collected character. We watched what the girls were doing. They had cut up lots of paper into small squares and written the words 'YES' and 'NO' and all the letters of the alphabet and the numbers one to ten on them and spread them around the edges of the table. In the centre of the table was a single beer glass. They all put one finger on the glass and linked hands around the table. Then Jane said, 'Is there anyone there?' The others gazed seriously at the glass.

'What are you doing?' I asked.

'Can't you shut up?' Jane shouted. 'We are trying to have a séance.'

Maria and I looked at each other.

'A what?' Maria asked.

One girl said, 'Instead of disturbing us, why don't you join in?'

'That's my sister Carol,' Jane said, looking at Maria. 'She's a bitch as well.'

The sister poked her tongue out and blew a raspberry at Jane. Carol was about the same age as Maria, but built along the heavier lines of her sister Jane.

We sat down.

Carol explained, 'Just rest your index finger lightly on the glass – do not put any pressure on it, none at all, OK? If we are lucky we will get a ghost.'

'You are all mad,' I said, but we put our fingers on the glass and linked hands.

Carol took the lead from her sister. 'Is there anyone there?' she asked.

The glass stayed exactly where it was. With Maria's hand in mine I rubbed her thigh, then she rubbed mine. Jane's foot came up from the other side of the table and she rubbed the inside of my thigh with her big toe. When she went higher she encountered our linked hands. The two girls stared at each other in defiance.

'Dirty cow!' said Maria.

'Little slut!' said Jane.

I opened my mouth to say something but Jane got there

first. 'Cradle snatcher! Why don't you get yourself a real woman instead of a little girl,' she sneered.

Maria went to get up but was stopped by Carol.

'For Christ's sake,' she hissed. 'How the hell are we supposed to get any spirits when you lot are shouting at each other. Just shut up, sit down, hold hands and bloody well concentrate or you can leave this house right now!'

'Yeah, shut up for Christ's sake!' added Judith. 'Pubescent children!'

Everyone put their fingers back on the glass again.

'Is there anybody there?' Carol asked.

Nothing happened.

'Is there anybody there?'

Nothing.

Then . . . It is very difficult to put down what exactly happened. Just for a few seconds, just for a moment, something crept into that bungalow. Something came softly in and took over the atmosphere of the room. The room was invaded. The hairs on the back of my neck and on my arms slowly stood up and my entire body was covered in goose-bumps. I looked at the others. They had noticed something as well, they were suddenly very serious. Sweat ran down Carol's face, and Maria's hand in mine was damp and clammy with sweat.

'Is there anybody there?' Carol demanded in a scratchy voice.

The glass wobbled from side to side.

'Stop doing that,' Maria said quietly to Jane.

Jane took her finger off and the glass still rocked slowly on its rim. She put her finger back on and the glass slid very slowly across the table towards me. It hesitated, then slid towards Carol. It stopped at the slip of paper with 'YES' written on it. Everyone accused each other of moving the glass and everyone denied it.

'Shut up!' Carol ordered. Then she asked, 'Who are you?'

The glass slid smoothly across the table. Something seemed to clamp my finger to it like glue. It went quickly from one letter to the next and spelt the word:

SORRY

I looked at the others. They were as terrified as me. We all knew by now that it wasn't one of us moving that glass. Carol was breathing tightly, her tongue moving over her lips, her eyes shining.

'Is that your name?' she asked.

NO

'What is your name?'

SORRY

'Why are you sorry?'

SAD

'Why are you sad?'

DEAD

'You are sorry because you are dead?'

NO

'You are not dead?'

The table suddenly rocked from a terrific impact and we all jumped backwards.

'Who did that!' shouted Jane.

Maria put her arm around me.

'I'm frightened, let's go, please,' she said.

Everybody was shouting and accusing each other of things again. Carol shut everyone up and made us put our fingers back on the glass.

'In a while we can go,' I whispered to Maria.

'Why are you sorry?' Carol asked and the glass moved directly.

MANY DEAD

'Where?'

HERE

'I don't understand? Dead here?'

YES CHILD WOMAN MAN SORRY

'There is nobody here . . . only us.'

BEFORE

'When before?'

SICK CHILD SORRY

'There was a sick child?'

MANY DEAD

'How many dead?'

The glass seemed to gain power under our fingers and did two fast, smooth circuits of the table. Maria said to Carol, 'Stop it please . . . I'm frightened.'

But Carol gave her a murderous look and repeated, 'How many dead?'

The glass went to the numbers and spelt out:

3 5 0

'Three hundred and fifty what? Dead people?'

YES

We all stopped breathing for as long as we could. Maria's hand was shaking. The girl I didn't know suddenly screamed and rushed out of the room. The rest of us kept our fingers on the glass. Nobody asked a question, but it moved anyway.

SORRY WAR

'The Second World War? What happened?'

YES

'What happened?' Carol insisted.

NO

'Tell us what happened!'

HOSPITAL SICK HERE DEAD

'People from the hospital were brought here and they died?'

YES

'How did they die?'

I KILL I SORRY

'You killed the people?'

YES NO AIR

'You killed three hundred and fifty people? Women and children?'

YES HERE ROOM

'In this room?'

YES

'Oh God!' said Carol. Maria's whole body was trembling.
'How did you kill them?' I asked.
The glass did nothing.
'How did you kill them?' Carol asked.
The glass moved.

ALL HERE TOGETHER

'Three hundred and fifty people in this one room at the same time?'

YES SICK NO AIR

MANY DEAD SORRY

'Everybody died?'

NO I KILL MANY

'How?'

NO

'How?'
The glass did not move.
'What is your name?'

Y A S U T O

'Are you Japanese?'

    YES

'Where are you now?'

    I N O T

'You are not what?'

    N O T

'Are you in hell?'

    N O T

Now the glass was moving very fast, as if confused.
'Is there a God?' I asked.
Very fast the glass spelled out,

    I K N O W

'Yes or no?' I asked.

    I K N O W

'Have you seen God?'

    I K N O W

'Can we see you?' Carol asked.

    YES

'How?'

    G L A S S

Carol looked at all of us.
'Take all your fingers off the glass as soon as I ask the question.'
'Can you show us?' she asked.
We all took our fingers off and watched. The atmosphere in the room was heavy and frightening. The glass rocked slightly on its rim, then it moved, just an inch and stopped. We all stopped breathing. It moved again, its rim scratching

slightly on the surface of the table, it gained speed and dashed from letter to letter:

H B I O T Z I U R E 6 8 I 3 5 B B N

S O R R Y I K N O W D E A D

It stopped. There was nothing in the room, we could have all been 2,000-year-old corpses. Suddenly Jane jumped to her feet and screamed, 'You dirty murdering bastard! You Jap pig . . . You . . . '

The glass tore across the table and fell to the floor with a loud smash.

I looked around the table. Everyone was white and shaking. Maria looked the worst, her eyes lost in her head. Carol stood up and vomited all over herself. The girl who had run out earlier came back out of the bedroom and said to Judith, 'Let's go. I can't stay here.'

They were gone. I took Maria out onto the balcony and filled her up with a big whisky. Jane and Carol came out and joined us.

'I can't stay here tonight,' Carol announced.

Jane agreed with her, then asked us, 'Did you believe that . . . what just happened. I think we dreamed it. It can't be true.'

'I don't know what to believe. But I do know I'm very frightened,' I said.

They all nodded their heads.

'I can't stay here either,' I said.

All three girls looked at me.

'We can't go to my house.' Maria pointed out.

'But I live on an island,' I said.

'Anywhere is better than here,' Carol said.

'Let's just get the hell out of here!' Carol added.

We left the house exactly as it was, apart from pushing the shutters closed on the room and locking the doors. I walked ahead and they followed like a flock of sheep until we got outside the BMH on the main road.

'What do we do now, walk?' Maria asked.

I waved my hand up and down the empty road.

'If you stand at the side of the road anywhere in Singapore at any time a Changi bus will come by sooner or later. It is an unwritten rule,' I assured all three of them.

They sat down on the kerb. I watched the road. Ten minutes later a Changi bus came screaming towards us with no lights on. I held my hand up and the driver slammed the brakes on and skidded to an impressive halt on the wrong side of the road.

'Your Changi bus, ladies,' I said.

They stared in amazement, then followed me on board. The driver was a ghostly figure in his darkened cab.

'Jardine Steps?' I asked through the glass partition. He gave a grunt and off we went. He drove hard and fast with all the lights off and we bounced about on the hard wooden seats. It could have been a journey to nowhere, rushing through the deserted streets at breathtaking speed. When I looked behind I imagined a form following us through the night air, its big black wings spread out and advancing on us like a locomotive out of control. The girls were also looking over their shoulders. There was a feeling of panic in the flight of the Changi bus, as though whatever we were running away from was either waiting for us at the end of the journey or was just outside the window if we dared to look.

The bus stopped, suddenly, and we were at Jardine Steps. I offered the driver a dollar, after taking it from Jane, but he grunted and was already engaging the gears so we jumped off and he sped away into the indifferent night. I thought we all might have to sleep on the jetty waiting for the six o'clock ferry, but after an hour some fishermen I knew came by and I hailed them down and they took us over to the island. To have landed at the jetty would have been foolish – the guards would have told my father – so I got the fishermen to drop us off at the small private beach and we waded the last bit with the water up to our chests.

'What do we do now?' asked Carol.

Maria was exhausted, too tired for anything but sleep; Jane was a shadowy form with flashing eyes sat down in the darkness.

'We stay here,' I said. 'There is a small hut where we can

sleep . . . It will be bloody swarming with mosquitoes but better than sleeping out in the open.'

It was pitch dark, absolute blackness. I had a job to see anything in front of me, and as we made our way across the beach I stumbled into one of the girls. She quickly grabbed me and kissed me hard on the lips. I didn't have a clue who it was, then realised that it couldn't be Maria because kissing was 'yukky'. She broke away with a giggle. We found the hut and I found Maria and we laid down together on the sand. The other two were very close, I could hear their breathing. Somehow we all fell asleep. I don't know about the others but I had terrible nightmares the minute my eyes closed, and every twenty minutes or so I woke up sweating and shivering. Eventually I left the hut and walked into the sea and sat in the cool, shallow water. Shadows moved against the dark vegetation behind me, monsters lurked there and in the corners of my brain. Then one of the shadows really moved and skittered down the beach towards me. For a second I was frozen with fear, then the shadow materialised into the form of Carol. She sat down with me.

'I couldn't sleep,' she said.

'Nor could I.'

'Hold my hand?' she asked. 'I'm frightened.'

I did.

In the very near distance something bobbed in the blackness of the sea.

'What's that?' she asked.

I looked, then remembered what it was.

'A raft,' I told her.

'Let's swim out to it,' she suggested.

We did, after she had stripped to her pants. Even in the darkness I could see she was wearing Jane's breasts.

It was only about forty feet out. It was one of those rafts like a giant tyre but made from cork, so you could climb inside and lay with your back against the sides with the water up to your chest. We were resting like that, opposite one another, when her legs came up and circled my hips.

'Were you frightened in the house?' she asked.

'Terrified,' I admitted.

'Are you frightened now?' she asked, and tightened her legs round me.

'No.'

'Good.'

She kept her thighs around me. We didn't speak for a few minutes.

'My sister told me all about you,' she said eventually.

'What did she say?'

'That you couldn't get a hard-on.'

'I was drunk.'

'Are you drunk now?'

'No.'

'Prove it then,' she said.

I liked Maria a hell of a lot, so much so that I wanted to say no, but when I opened my mouth different words came out.

'OK. As long as you don't tell Maria.'

'Why are you so worried about Maria? She's just a kid.'

'She's the same age as you,' I pointed out.

'No she's not! I'm a year older!'

'Will you keep your mouth shut or not?' I asked.

'Why?'

'I like Maria . . . a lot.'

'You'll like me better, all the boys do. But I won't say anything. Don't worry about your precious Maria.'

I grunted.

'Was that you?' she asked.

'Me what?'

'That touched me on my thigh?'

'No.'

'Shit!' she screamed and leaped out of the water onto the raft.

'What's wrong?' I asked.

'Get out quick!' she shouted. 'I think it's a sea-snake!'

I stayed where I was. Sea-snakes are not dangerous as long as you keep still. I knew that from Richard. Their gape is tiny and they usually cannot get to grips with anything as large as a human being – though if they do you are unquestionably dead. After two minutes I climbed casually up onto the raft with Carol.

We took our few remaining clothes off and knelt down facing each other. I went to push her onto her back but she stopped me.

'No, you lay down,' she said.

'Why?' I asked.

'Don't ask stupid questions! Just do it!'

I laid down.

'I meant on your back, you stupid bastard, not on your stomach. Christ!'

I turned over and she scrambled on top of me. She felt me.

'That's good, that's very good. Now just relax, I'll do everything, OK?'

'Yeah.'

'And when you fire, tell me, OK? I like to know when you fire, that's the best bit.'

'Fire?' I asked.

'Yeah, fire. Make sure you tell me when you're ready to fire. And don't fire until I'm ready.'

I still didn't have a clue what she was on about, but she started lowering herself onto me and I forgot all about it. No girl had ever done stuff like this to me before.

After a couple of minutes she started moving faster and her breath was coming hard.

'Are . . . you . . . ready . . . yet?' she asked between funny little noises.

'Ready? Ready for what?' I asked.

'To fire! Come on! I'm ready for Christ's sake. Fire!' she shouted.

'What do . . . ?'

She was going faster and faster.

'Fire you bastard!' she demanded. 'Fire! Fire! Now!'

'I don't know . . . '

'Shut up and fire!' she screamed. 'Now! Christ! Why don't you fire? I'm ready!' Then she groaned and shuddered and ground herself against me.

After she'd finished she said in a croaky voice, 'Shit, you missed it.'

She laid down on top of me breathing like a runaway lunatic. Then she sat up again.

'Why didn't you fire?' she demanded.

'I don't know what you're talking about, Carol!'

'You were supposed to fire when I was ready! Why didn't you?'

'What do you mean, *fire*?' I asked. I was honestly confused.

She looked at me. 'You know what I mean . . . come. Why didn't you come in me? I like it.'

'Come?' I asked.

'Oh God! Have I got to spell it out? Why didn't you shoot your sperm into me?'

'Oh,' I said. Now I knew what she meant.

'Well, why not?' she demanded.

'I err . . . well, I don't actually. I mean I haven't . . . '

'You can't come?' she asked.

'I get a feeling, but nothing comes out,' I explained.

'Jesus, what a wimp! How old are you?'

'Fifteen.'

'And you still don't come? Shit, I've done it with twelve-year-olds who can fire, good and proper. There's no fun in it if you can't fire.'

'I get enough fun out of it,' I told her.

'Christ! You're still in your puberty!'

'It was your idea to do it anyway. I couldn't care less!'

'At the least I thought I was getting a man, not some pubescent little boy!'

I slipped back into the water.

'What are you doing?' she demanded,

'Going back to the beach.'

'No you are bloody well not! You are not leaving me alone on this raft!'

'Come back with me then,' I said, and started to swim with slow, even strokes.

'Bastard!' she shouted.

As I was wading up to the beach, Jane appeared suddenly out of the darkness and shoved me back into the water.

'You are like a dog!' she hissed.

And then she was on top of me, thumping, kicking, biting and scratching. She was strong and I had to really fight hard to get her off.

She sat in the water and looked at me.

'First it was some bloody baboon, then your Maria and now my shitty sister. I could hear you from here, her and her bloody "Fire". She's a nymphomaniac, you know that?'

'I never touched her.'

'Like hell you didn't!'

Maria came running up.

'What happened?' she asked. 'I heard shouting.'

Jane was just about to open her mouth when the bushes at the side of the beach erupted as though an elephant was charging through them. Both girls leaped on me, digging their nails into my skin in their fright.

'What is it?' Maria screamed.

'Shut up!' I shouted. I was just as frightened as them. I brought my fingers up to my lips and gave three piercing whistles that shattered the night. The lumbering crashing noises continued to come from the bushes. Ten seconds passed, twenty seconds . . . Then came the sound of animals racing frantically across the soft sand, and the girls dug their nails even harder into my skin. A blood-curdling series of pants and growls rumbled towards us, then Rape and Pillage materialised out of the dark and jumped up and down on me. I pointed to the bushes and shouted to the dogs, 'There! Go!'

They were off, hurtling over the sand and tearing into the bushes. The crashing noise stopped. Then there was a terrific howl and the dogs came running back to my side in a maelstrom of fur and sand.

'It's all right,' I said to the two girls. 'It's only some iguanas.'

'How do you know that?' Maria asked.

I patted both dogs on their heads.

'There is nothing else on this planet they would run away from. They know not to hurt iguanas – I taught them.'

'Thank Christ for that,' Jane said.

We all sat there in the shallow water playing with the dogs. After a while Carol started hollering from the raft.

'What's she doing out there?' Maria asked.

'Ask your boyfriend,' Jane said.

'She went for a swim,' I explained.

It was no longer so dark now, as a weak dawn began to warm the sky. I got the canoe and paddled over to the raft and collected Carol.

'Bastard!' she complained.

'You can shut up as well,' I said, prodding her with the paddle.

'Did you manage to give Maria one. I'm better aren't I? Admit it. You loved it.'

'Shut up!' I told her, and hit her harder with the paddle.

'Ouch!'

When I got her back on the beach all three girls started to complain.

'I'm hungry.'

'I'm thirsty.'

'I need a toilet.'

'I want to have a shower.'

'I need to clean my teeth.'

'Oh sweet suffering Jesus!' I groaned. Sometimes it was just not worth it. They kept on and on. I reckoned it must still have been only five in the morning and I knew nobody would be up until at least eight, so after making them all promise to keep quiet I led the pack up towards our bungalow on the hill. The place seemed deserted. I sent the dogs back to their sleeping place on the front balcony to avoid any accidents with them. Outside the bungalow were a row of small buildings where the amah had her bedroom, washing room, shower and toilet, and I let the girls go in there and do all the things they wanted to do. Our kitchen was also outside. I crept in, rummaged about in the big fridge, and found orange juice, Shitbag, who yawned very loudly and went back to sleep, and some cheese. Maria and I sat on the big steps between the bungalow and the amah's rooms eating and drinking. There was a slight noise from behind us and I turned to see our amah staring at us out of her half-open bedroom door. I brought my finger up to my lip in the sign of silence, and she smiled and shut the door. Carol came out of the shower and sat down with us.

'Smashing,' she said, stuffing cheese and orange juice into herself.

The main door of the house opened and mother stood there in her nightdress, blinking at us.

'Good morning, mother,' I called.

She blinked a little more rapidly.

'Who are those people?' she asked.

'Maria and Carol. They came over with me on the early morning ferry. We're all going swimming,' I explained.

Jane walked nonchalantly out of the shower room with a towel around her waist and her bare breasts wobbling dramatically.

'Good morning,' she called out cheerfully to my mother, and went into the washing room to get dressed.

'And what was that?' asked mother.

'Ah,' I said. It was all I could think of.

'Your father will give you "Ah" if he wakes up and comes out here and finds you with a bunch of half-naked girls.'

More information than that I didn't need. I rustled the three girls up and pushed them lickety-split down the hill away from the house, while they all protested like hell. Once the house was out of sight I slowed down.

'What's the rush?' Jane asked. 'I didn't have any breakfast.'

'Did you ever meet my father?' I asked.

They all shook their heads.

'He is the rush.'

I walked on ahead. Jane caught up with me. Carol and Maria were walking together. Under any other circumstances it would have been a wonderful early morning walk – the air was fresh, birds were singing, and Singapore at that time in the morning was a dream – but I had the feeling that something bad was in the wind. Jane confirmed that.

'Carol is explaining to your darling Maria what happened on your little swim out to the raft,' she told me.

'You love it don't you?' I said. 'The chance to get at me, you just love it.'

'Too bloody right I do. Just who the hell do you think you are?'

'You are just plain, ordinary, bloody jealous!'

'Of you? Don't make me bloody laugh. You can't even come! She told me.'

'Fuck you, Jane.'

'If only you could, but you can't even do that, can you?'

'Jane. I happen to like Maria a hell of a lot. If you and your sister want to cock that up, then go ahead.'

'Why did you screw my sister then?' she demanded.

'Oh Christ, I don't know.'

Maria came between us and touched my arm.

'I want to talk to you,' she said. 'Alone.'

'Good luck,' said Carol as she passed us.

'Did you do it with Carol last night?' Maria asked.

She looked so perfect that I could have jumped in her eyes and stayed there forever.

'Yes.'

'Why?'

'I don't know.'

'Fuck you!' she said, and ran off to join the other two. I looked at the road and thought about beating my head in on its hard surface.

I followed them instead. On the way to the jetty we passed Richard's house, and he was leaning over the wall with a pair of fighting cocks tied around his neck. He watched the three girls walk past and then me bringing up the rear. He gave me a look which said 'I told you so' and shook his head. I was beginning to think that he was right. Girls were bad for your health.

They got on the ferry without even looking at me and I never saw Maria again.

But there is a sequel: sadly not Maria coming back and saying all is forgiven. No, a really boring sequel. I found out that during the war about three hundred and fifty people were dragged out of their hospital beds and stuffed inside the house where we had the séance and suffocated by the Japs. Any who didn't die of lack of breath were shot or stuck through with a bayonet. So that was a fact, and we had our little séance and some Jap came back and wanted to be forgiven for wiping out a load of kids, women and sick men. I didn't forgive him. Maria didn't forgive me. But that's all in the past, isn't it? Just like me being a pimp. And who is going to forgive me for that? What the hell, life goes on. But then I lost Richard. That was bad. I mean, how can someone like Richard just up and say, 'I'm off'? He did. He put his hand in mine, threw his arm around my shoulders and broke all my bones and said, 'You're a guy. I love you so much I could break all the bones in your body.'

Then he got on a flight for Thailand and left. He had no idea how long he would be away – perhaps a week, a month, maybe a year.

Bad times: no Richard; no Maria.

10

It was and it is my life, and if I want to go around making a major mess of it then that is my own problem. The one thing I never looked for, now or then, was sympathy. I needed that like a hole in the head. I had few friends and I reckon Maria could have been another . . . Call it what you like, we would have had a good time. But I've always been absolutely brilliant at throwing things away and bloody useless at keeping them. Like with that toad the Boss. If I'd just kept my nose clean I'd have been set up for life: Range Rover, air-conditioned mansion, servants, two horses, twelve dogs, so much money that I could buy a speedboat and forget that I owned it . . . Then I have to go and stage a gigantic wobbler and start running around with an automatic weapon and threatening to blow people away, get involved with very bad news people, and so on and so on.

I've been on the move since the day I was born: half a year in India , two years in Hong Kong, a year in England, another year in Hong Kong . . . Friendships don't mean so much when you're always moving on, and nor do possessions. You learn to travel hard and fast and you learn to be on your own. Give me a good dog, enough alcohol and an island, then I'm happy.

With Richard gone for an indefinite period, which was to turn into that disgusting word forever, I didn't have anywhere else to stay except at home. This wasn't a big success. My appearance and manner deteriorated to such an appalling extent that my mother refused to have me at the table, or anywhere near when there were guests. My dinner used to go to Shitbag, Rape and Pillage – they were really happy with that. I wasn't happy there full stop. Dave was hardly ever there, but spent most of his time in Singapore in the company of an absolutely gorgeous brigadier's daughter who had rescued his despicable remains from a monsoon ditch (favourite spot of his) one night and convinced him to clean up his act. At least when Dave was there we could have a laugh.

I took to living almost full time in an old deserted bunker at the top of the highest hill on the island. It had been built by the British before the Second World War and then enlarged by the Japanese when they conquered the island. It was a vast underground complex with tunnels leading all over the island, and was reputed even to have a tunnel link with Blakamati, the Island of the Dead. I did find one long tunnel and explored it for about five hundred yards but gave up in fright when I discovered it was full of snakes. I found the shed skin of a large cobra and kept it. One day I showed it to Rape and Pillage and they both did standing leaps of five feet with their hair stood on end, then disappeared at a million miles an hour with their tails tucked between their legs. A cobra skin is the best protection in the world against rabid dogs. I never saw Rape or Pillage frightened of anything else.

The place was full of ruined buildings, above the ground as well as below, and in one of these I had my sleeping place on an old stone bench. The dogs slept either side of me, their throaty breathing and warmth a sacred charm against the dark nights.

To me the place was a palace – it even had fresh running water supplied by an old water tower, which also provided an ideal lookout point. The whole island could be watched from up there, as could a good deal of mainland Singapore.(This was before Mr Lee Kuan Facking Yew devastated the skyline of the country.) I used to sit with my arms around Rape and Pillage, quietly watching the sinking sun covering the hills and trees in blood.

In the trees nearby were the nests of a flock of crows and

they became good friends. I could call up early in the mornings from the top of the tower and they would wheel around my head in untidy circles, like a pack of scruffy playing cards tossed into the wind.

I climbed up to one of the nests and found a young crow and hijacked him. After a little while he wouldn't leave me, sitting on my shoulder and flapping around my ears if I took a walk anywhere. Whenever I lit a fire he would throw himself onto the flames in ecstasy, and if I hadn't pushed him out he would have burned himself to death. I could see that we had a lot in common.

Sometimes I went down to Ma Lee's house to eat, but most of the time I lived off the fish I caught and fruit I scrounged or found – there were a lot of breadfruit and papaya trees on the island, and bananas and coconuts were there for the picking. The dogs used to go home and eat, or scrounge fish off me. It was just the sort of wild, remote life I was looking for.

In one of the underground bunkers I found a conveyor belt that still worked. It turned by hand and was obviously built during the war to ferry ammunition from the bunker up to the big guns that were once dug in at the top of the complex. Open metal boxes big enough to take a large shell were fastened to the belt. The first time I cranked the machine by turning the rusty old hand mechanism, the belt creaked tight against the rust; but I finally moved it by hanging on the lever with all my body weight. I turned the lever for a while, watching the empty metal boxes disappearing out of the hole in the bunker roof, then made the dogs sit in two of the boxes and gave them a ride to the surface. They both rushed back down again for another go and it became one of our favourite games during that time.

It was well known on the island that I had made my home in the old bunker complex and I had very few visitors in the time I was there. The combination of a pair of supposedly vicious dogs and a raving maniac with rabies kept nearly everybody at a good distance. Sometimes a gang of kids from the kampong tried to have a look, but I always saw or heard them when they were a long way off and ambushed them with the dogs or catapulted stones at them from the top of the water tower.

It was a very spooky place, especially at night. Before I took up residence there, it had been left almost as the British Army found it when they liberated Singapore from the Japanese. There were many unhappy spirits inhabiting the tunnels, where I'm sure soldiers from both sides had died. I thought perhaps there might be some buried treasure as well, and spent many days and weeks exploring every foot of the place, under and above the ground. My dream was to find a machine gun wrapped in oiled cloth and in perfect working order, and a heavy belt of ammunition. I could set it up on top of the tower, run a flag up and declare the Independent State of the Island; then I'd send a string of totally outrageous and unreasonable demands to Mr Lee Kuan Facking Yew.

After some weeks I had dug over all of the floors and searched through most of the tunnels, but the only treasure I found was a rusty old pistol. It was so rotted that it would never work, but I carried it around with me anyway.

Not so long after finding the pistol, I was excavating the floor space in the biggest bunker, where the conveyor belt was located, when I heard strange noises from above. The dogs stood stock still, listening and growling very low. I motioned them to stop. Someone was walking around on the upper level of the bunker. I made the dogs get into the metal boxes of the conveyor and slowly wound them up to the surface. The belt creaked and groaned a little, but whoever was up there probably didn't hear it.

I figured that the sight of two vicious dogs emerging on a conveyor belt out of the bowels of the earth would scare the hell out of anybody. It did.

There was a startled scream from above, followed by the barking of the dogs and the sound of running feet. The dogs were at the base of the water tower, when I reached the surface, barking and trying to leap up the rungs of the ladder. Whoever it was had done the right thing to get away from them – climbed up the tower where they couldn't follow. In the tower was a whole complex of further chambers and rooms, and whoever it was had hidden in one of those. I picked up Rape and put him across my shoulder. He bit me a couple of times in his excitement, but once he tasted who it was he left off. On the first storey I let him down and he threw himself against a closed wooden door, trying to rip the handle out with his teeth and scratching against it with his claws. I called him back and made him sit by the ladder.

I pushed the door slowly open and in the darkness could just make out the form of someone in the far corner. Whoever it was turned, and though I still couldn't see well enough to make this person out, he or she could see me clearly against the light of the open door.

'Christ!' a girl exclaimed. 'You have got even worse.'

It was none other than Judith, the infamous girl from the infamous party.

I didn't say anything. She moved to the door.

'Is it safe to come out?' she asked.

'Slowly,' I told her.

As she emerged I told the dog to be still. At that moment my pet crow appeared from nowhere and landed on my shoulder with a loud *kraww*.

She jumped back in the doorway.

'What the hell is that?'

'My bird.'

She came back out and looked me up and down.

'God! Look at the state of you.'

'What's wrong with me?' I asked.

'Your hair is over your shoulders and filthy. You look like a girl. When was the last time you took a shower – you stink. You smell like a disembowelled wombat!'

She noticed the old pistol tied to my belt.

'And,' she pointed out, 'you are wearing a gun.'

'What the hell are you doing here, Judith?'

She smiled. 'I came over to your brother's birthday party. Remember your brother, Dave?'

I grunted. I'd been up at the tower for ages and hadn't seen my brother once.

'I was talking to Jane at the party. You do remember sweet Jane, don't you? The girl you were going to do it with on Blakamati?'

'Yeah, I remember Jane. What was she doing at my brother's birthday party?'

'Dave and her are going out together now. But you wouldn't know anything about that, locked up here in your little fort playing Tarzan, would you?'

'I thought he was going out with some brigadier's daughter?'

'He was, until the brigadier found out.'

'What do you want, Judith?'

She started down the ladder.

'Is the other dog OK?' she shouted out.

'No,' I answered. She stopped, then climbed back up.

I took the dog on my shoulder, the crow flew off, and I climbed down. She followed me down. I could see straight up her dress. She had nothing on underneath. For all my self-imposed monkhood, I found it exciting.

The dogs went off to sniff around, once I had told them both to relax.

'Where do you sleep?' she asked.

She followed me. I pushed the door open and she walked in, looked at my stone bed with its one old blanket, and sat down. Judith was a very good-looking girl in a cheeky sort of way.

'Did you like it?' she asked.

I already knew what she meant, but pretended I didn't. 'Like what?' I asked.

'Looking up my dress. Did you like what you saw?'

'Why don't you wear pants, Judith?'

'See! You did look!'

'I could hardly help it.'

'I do wear pants sometimes, like at school, but I took them off before coming up here.'

'Why did you come up here, Judith?'

She laid back against the wall and pulled her dress slowly over her thighs and up until it was over her waist. There was something totally erotic about her sitting like that in the broken, dirty old bunker.

'Do it to me,' she ordered.

Christ, I wanted to, but it was bloody embarrassing. My face was glowing like a 300-watt lightbulb.

'Jane told me, so did Carol,' she said, wriggling about on the stone.

'What did they tell you?'

'That you can't come. I haven't done it without a Durex for months. I hate the bloody things, but if I get pregnant one more time my father will send me back to England, for good. You are perfect. Come on!'

I turned my back on her. Jesus, it was embarrassing the way some people talked about sex. At that age I was mega-sensitive about such things, and ever since the episode with Carol had been wondering why I still didn't 'fire'. In fact I had cultivated quite a tidy little complex about it.

'Come on, Tarzan!' she urged.

I turned back and faced her. God! She looked incredibly desirable. I'd give everything I have left in the world for her to be sat in my hotel room with her dress up around her waist telling me to 'Come on!' right now.

'I don't like the fact that I can't come,' I told her.

'I love it, dingbat. Get over here.'

'Christ, Judith, I can't just screw to order.'

'You screwed Carol, didn't you?' she asked.

'Yeah.'

'You screwed Maria, didn't you?'

'Yeah.'

'Then get over here and bloody well screw me!'

I shook my head.

'I don't have crabs or anything any more. Do it to me! *Do* me now!'

'I can't,' I whispered.

'DO ME!' she screamed.

I turned away from her, shaking my head, and looked out of the door.

'Come on, Tarzan. Are you a man or what? You're supposed to be so bloody tough, but you're just a frightened kid, too frightened to screw, too frightened to give me one. Bloody child! If you don't do it to me, I'll tell all the other girls that you not only can't come, I'll tell them that you only

135

have a two-inch dick. I'll tell everyone that you are a little poof, a little fairy. I'll tell . . . '

She never finished because something just snapped and I went crazy and attacked her. Not sexually. I wanted to hurt her, bad. I wanted to knock Jane out of her and Carol out of her and Maria out of her, and shut her mouth.

We ended up on the floor like a pair of raving baboons, scratching, slapping and thumping each other. The dogs burst in and attacked us both – confused as to what to do, they just slashed out with their teeth. Judith's dress was ripped to shreds and we both had bites and scratches all over the place and then her hands pulled my shorts down and we were doing it before we realised what was going on. The dogs backed off and there was silence apart from our frantic breathing. It was brutal, hard stuff – not sex, more like revenge. Then I 'fired'. I couldn't believe it, just like that. Along with the usual feeling was a stream of stuff. I had my very first real orgasm. I don't know what Judith had, but it was something like an epileptic fit.

'Christ,' she said. 'You just raped me.'

She certainly looked that way, her dress hanging around her in tatters and blood oozing out of a lot of dog bites and mingling with all the dirt on her skin from the floor. I didn't look any better, but then I never did.

She sat on the bench, brushing grit off her arms and legs.

'Look at the state of me . . . What am I going to say to Chris?'

'Who is Chris?' I asked.

'My boyfriend, he's at the party.'

'You'll think of something, Judith.'

'Christ!' she screamed looking down between her legs. 'What the bloody hell is that?'

'What?' I asked, startled by her outburst.

'Bastard! Oh, you slimy bastard . . . You came in me, you bastard!'

'Oh,' I said.

'Shit! I only did it with you because you couldn't come and now look what you've done, you stupid boy. Oh God, I'm probably pregnant again. Why did you do that?'

'I didn't know I was going to come.'

'Well you bloody well should have known.'

'You know what, Judith?' I asked.

She stopped looking down at herself, 'What?' she demanded. Her face was screwed up like a pixie who finds someone has trampled her ring to pieces.

'I give up . . . I really give up. I can't do anything right. When I don't come you all take the piss out of me. When I do come you shout and swear at me. You can all fuck off!'

'I'd better not be pregnant, you bastard!'

'You can blame one of the many others for it if you are.'

'No I can't! They all use things.'

I walked out of the door and stood outside in the sunlight. Rape and Pillage grinned at me, wagging their tails. They thought all this was great fun. Sod it! I was thinking. I am never going near a girl again for as long as I live. A minute later she came out and shoved me in the back, hard. I thought she was still mad but she was smiling.

'Hey, I didn't mean to shout at you and call you names. I was just bloody angry. I wasn't expecting it, that's all. It wasn't your fault. It's like Milne said,' she said.

'What did Milne say?' I asked, though I really wanted to say, 'Who the hell is Milne?'

' "It's like this," he said. "When you go after honey with a balloon, the great thing is not to let the bees know you're coming." '

She laughed and I gave her my best small schoolboy grin.

'In fact,' she said, 'I think it is cause for celebration.'

'What do you mean, celebration?' I asked.

'What do you think, Tarzan?' and she pulled me by the hand back into the room.

'What about getting pregnant?'

'Stuff all that. It felt so good without that disgusting rubber thing.'

'I don't know whether I can,' I said.

'Oh, you can, Tarzan, you can,' she said, and she was right. As soon as we had finished she looked at her watch.

'Christ, I gotta go. Wait till I tell Jane and the others about this!'

'You don't have to tell anyone about it,' I said.

'Are you kidding? I tell who I like, sunshine. I'm the same as you. I do just what I bloody well like.'

She leaned over and kissed me lightly on the cheek. 'Bye, Tarzan,' she said.

'Say hi to Dave for me,' I said as she walked out of the door.

She stopped and touched my arm.

'Why don't you come to Singapore some time? Come to some of the parties or the school dances, instead of shutting yourself away on this island like a mad hermit. You act like an old man. You're only fifteen, remember?'

'I like it here, with the dogs and stuff.'

'Grow up will you for Christ's sake. Get your hair cut and tidy yourself up a bit. Who knows, your parents might even let you back in the house. At least you could have a bath then. You have to go back to England in a few months time. Look at the state of you. Do you really think you can walk down Portsmouth High Street looking like that, with your one-eyed and one-eared dogs and that bloody black parrot on your shoulder and a pistol strapped to your filthy body?'

'It's a crow, Judith, not a parrot.'

'I don't care if it's a frigging golden eagle!' she shouted. 'Just grow up, will you?'

I stared at the ground. She put both her hands on my shoulders.

'Listen. If you come to the next school dance, I'll drop Chris and go out with you. We could do it every day if you came over to Singapore.'

'I don't want to come to Singapore, Judith.'

'Didn't you like what we just did or what?'

'Yeah, I liked it.'

She smiled. 'Good. If you won't come to Singapore, I'll come over here every so often and then we can do it and I can keep Chris as well. He's sweet.'

Then she skipped off, quite happy with herself. A practical girl.

Judith was true to her word. She started coming over to the

island – just once a week to start with, then it was twice a week . . . When she started coming over three times a week we realised that we wanted to see each other every day. She told me she'd given up Chris and all the others. I didn't really believe her – she was too damned practical. We realised that we liked each other a hell of a lot. Love was a word none of us ever used at that time. We all thought we would find out what love was later, when we grew up. We were too young, stupid and blind to know that what we had in those days in Singapore was the real thing, and that everything that came later would be different.

I suppose Judith was a slut. But I've always been fond of sluts; and if Judith was a slut, then what was I? Better a slut than a pimp . . . I found that out later. She laughed at everything and nothing made her change stride. The world could be consumed by a massive atomic explosion and she'd be worrying about her next period.

We did it like there was no tomorrow: up in the water tower, in the ammunition room, on the beach, in the water, in the jungle while being eaten alive by ants, anywhere and everywhere. I reckon Rape and Pillage could have explained the facts of life to any other dog lacking the vital knowledge – they were always there, panting and impatient to be off. This went on forever: a crazy time of urgent desires, hard young bodies, and a who-gives-a-damn attitude to everything and everyone. We were locked in a box, just the two of us; we had the keys and we thought it would never end, that nobody could ever stop it. I suppose we both realised that things would never be like this again.

Then came the first small earthquake in paradise. 'We have cause for another celebration,' Judith announced.

She hadn't been over for three days and I had been worrying about her.

'What?' I asked.

'Come on,' she said, and led me by the hand up the tower ladder.

'What's the celebration then?' I asked, once we were in the roofless room upstairs.

'I'm pregnant,' she said, and the ground tilted slightly under my feet.

'Oh,' I said. I'm really great at times like this. I always say something really relevant and dynamic.

'Yeah, your firing has proved to be accurate.'

'Oh.'

'I think you should say something like, "Oh Judith, whatever are we going to do?" don't you?'

'Judith, what are we going to do?' I asked.

'That's better,' she said, and slipped her shorts down over her hips. 'Now we don't have to worry about anything, do we?'

'Christ! Judith, aren't you worried about it?'

'Sure I am. But now is now and right now I want to feel you inside me. Come on, help me celebrate.'

It was crazy, like it could be the last time. Maybe we knew it was.

She was laid beneath me, her head rocking from side to side, biting on her tongue, when there was a sudden roaring and the room was enveloped in a cloud of choking dust. I stopped and looked up in horror. A dark green army helicopter was hanging right over the roofless room, its occupants staring down at us. I was about to jump off, but Judith grabbed me tight and shouted above the din of the rotor blades. 'Don't stop now for Christ's sake, I'm coming!'

The helicopter took off at speed, its rotors whump-whumping, and Judith said, 'God, that was great. The best yet.'

'Didn't you see that helicopter?'

'Sure I saw the stupid helicopter. Nosey bastards!'

'But they saw us doing it . . . '

'So what. They shouldn't be flying around in the air nosing into other people's business.'

'It's all right for you, it's not your problem. But whoever was in that helicopter probably knows me,' I explained.

'Not my problem! I'm pregnant because of you and all you worry about is that someone saw you at it. Don't make me sick.'

She had a point so I shut up. But I was still worried. There could have been anyone in that helicopter . . .

Another little earthquake in paradise.

We walked to the jetty in silence.

'What are you going to do?' I asked her on the jetty.

'I don't know.'

'You have to do something,' I said.

She turned and stared at me.

'Listen, Tarzan. This is my problem, OK? I don't want you to lose your beauty sleep over it. I'll do something. Christ knows what, but I'll manage. Probably have to go to England and visit my grandmother again.'

'Grandmother?' I asked.

She kissed me.

'Child, don't worry. For pleasures past I do not grieve, nor perils gathering near. My greatest grief is that I leave no thing that claims a tear. That's Byron.'

As the small ferry drew away from the jetty, she stood at the cabin door and gave me one single wave.

Was that a final goodbye? I worried all that night about it. I also wondered just who the hell was in the helicopter and what sort of shit I was going to be in.

I found out early the next morning.

Dave arrived at the bunker while I was burning a bit of fish on an open fire for breakfast. He bowed low and swept an imaginary cap off his head.

'Greetings, oh long lost mad brother of mine. I bring you news from the court of his Royal Imperial Highness, He Who Must Be Obeyed, Our Great Paternal Pater. The news is this: you are in the deepest shit possible after being seen engaged in an act of copulation with the delicious Judith. I needn't remind you that I was there before you and it was certainly worth the dose of crabs I inherited on that wonderful occasion. However, I was not seen by pater's airborne commanding officer with my white bum waving in the air like a flag of surrender. You were. It is my duty to escort you back to the house where a tribunal sits in order to try you for your wicked and sinful deeds.'

He sat down on the other side of the fire.

'What's the fish like?' he asked.

'Is he raving mad or just ordinary mad?' I asked.

Dave tore a big chunk of the fish off.

'The shit really hit the fan last night, but he's calmed down a bit now. He has decided that it is a waste of time shouting at you or trying to turn you into something that might resemble a second-born son. He just wants you at home until we leave so we can all keep an eye on you. This fish is really good.'

'And what if I ignore this summons?' I asked.

He spat a bone into the fire and waved his fish towards the drooling dogs stood nearby.

'They'll be shot, for a start,' he said.

'He wouldn't dare.'

'Don't you believe it. He is quite prepared to machine-gun them himself. Have you got any more fish?'

I shook my head.

'Pity. Did you know I'm head boy at school now?' he asked.

'You . . . Head boy? You have got to be joking!'

'I'm quite the little angel these days. It must be getting away from your evil influence.'

'Are you really going out with Jane?'I asked.

'I could say,"Are you really going out with Judith?" but I won't.'

'What happened to the brigadier's daughter?' I asked.

'Daddy caught us at it in the bedroom and when he found out that father is only a captain I was out on my ear. Pity, she was one hell of a girl.'

'What else?' I asked.

'What else what?'

'What else will father do if I don't come home?'

'Well, if you think about it, it is the only sensible thing to do. We all have to leave, apart from father, some time in the next two or three months, and you are going to have to find homes for Shitbag, Rape and Pillage. No, don't even say that you want to take them back to England. You know that's stupid. If you don't follow orders then father will see to it that you leave this week, and I know you would rather have two or three months on your island. Do you want a beer? I know it's early, but there's an alcohol ban in the house and I sneaked some cans out.'

He emptied a carrier bag full of cans onto the ground. We drank for a while.

'You never did it with Jane, did you?' he asked me.

'That's a long story.'

'I've got plenty of time.'

'Well, she was going to let me, but then the monkey happened along . . . '

'Father's favourite subject,' he said.

I nodded my head, 'And then I met Maria. And then I screwed her sister, which never goes down very well amongst sisters, so we never got round to it . . . '

'But do you think she was really going to let you? Or was it all talk?' he asked.

'I think she meant it,' I assured him.

'Did she ever show you her breasts?' he asked.

'Christ, yes! In the canoe. I nearly fell overboard. I think I could write a poem about her breasts.'

'Yeah, she has a pair of real beauties, and she likes to show them around . . . But she won't let me do it with her.'

'No?' I asked in surprise.

He shook his head sadly.

'I'll let you into a secret,' I told him. 'Bring her up here and take her down in the dark bunker and tell her that you once found a skeleton there, and I guarantee she won't be able to get her pants off quick enough.'

'Really?' he exclaimed.

'One hundred per cent,' I assured him.

'I'll try it tomorrow. If it works, I'll buy you a case of Tiger.'

We drank our beers for a while.

'You know that you won't be able to see Judith any more? Well, at least on the island,' he said.

I stared at the fire.

'Judith is pregnant,' I said.

'Holy shit!' he said, and dropped his beer.

'Yeah, holy shit is right.'

'Christ! I should have brought you a Bible instead of a beer, boy. You have some serious praying to do. Do you realise what father would do to you if he found that out?'

'Yeah, I realise.'

'Whatever you do, under no circumstances tell anyone. On my mother's deathbed I swear that he would shoot you and claim justifiable homicide.'

'I'm not going to tell anyone. But you know Judith, she has to tell the world about everything,' I said.

He shook his head and made clucking noises while he opened a new beer.

'You've put me right off sex, you know that? I think I'll leave Jane alone . . . You might as well have her. Oh boy, oh boy, you really are incredible. What's next? What wonderful stunt are you going to pull next?'

'I could always shoot Mr Lee Kuan Facking Yew?' I offered.

'Now that, my dear brother, is a very good idea.'

'Cheers,' I said, holding my beer up.

'Here's to life and all its mysteries,' he said.

'Do you think there are any left?' I asked.

'No. I reckon we have just about explored them all by now,' he answered, then added, 'Did anyone ever tell you that you stink?'

'Judith told me, yes.'

'I mean, did she tell you that you really smell bloody awful?' He paused. 'You coming home now?'

I nodded my head in agreement, and we walked down to the house together with our arms around each other's shoulders and Rape and Pillage happily waving their tails as they trotted along behind.

So there it was, back at home. Dave took me into the bathroom and pointed at a pile of new clothes and said, 'Shower.' The clothes were disgusting – sandals and white socks, white starched shirt and the baggiest pair of khaki shorts that the world has ever seen. When I was washed and dressed, and looking like Gandhi in a British Army uniform, Dave showed me into the dining room and sat me down on a single chair placed in the middle of the room, and left. An evil-looking one-eyed Chinaman came into the room and without a word pulled out a pair of scissors and started chopping my hair off. I recognised the bastard – he used to empty the shit buckets before we had flushing toilets, and was now the official barber. I would have liked to have jumped off the chair and punched him right in the mouth and then set the dogs on him, but I didn't. After ten minutes I was as close as you can get to being bald and he departed, satisfied with the result. Dave came back into the room and slipped the black-framed glasses that I had refused to wear for the last four years over my nose, then stood back and studied the result. 'You look wonderful, Mr Gandhi,' he said, and left again.

The big clock on the wall ticked away for at least ten minutes, and then father, in full uniform, walked in through the door. I jumped. With his arms behind his back he inspected me, walking around and around. Finally he stopped and tapped me with his stick. I jumped again.

'I want you to take a good look in the mirror because what you see is what you are going to see so long as you live under this roof. There is much I could say, especially concerning the events of yesterday . . . ' All this had been said in a normal voice but then he crouched down suddenly and whispered in my ear, *'I'd like to rip your head off, you little bastard!'*

'But we, your mother and I, have decided' – this was in his normal voice again – 'to give you this last chance. You are not to leave the island, you are not to have any girl visitors, and before you leave the house you have to let your mother know where you are going. When I am away you will continue to act as if I am here. Is that understood?'

I nodded my head.

'Any infringement and your feet will not touch the ground. We'll have you put on an aeroplane to England, the same day.' He leant down to my ear again. *'And I'll personally beat you to death,*' he whispered. 'Now go to your room and read!' he shouted.

Talk about bad! Mother wouldn't talk to me, at all, for ages. She really took sexual misbehaviour seriously. One time she caught Dave in bed with a girl and she wouldn't let him eat for a whole month. He had to sleep without sheets as well, because she tore them off the bed and threw them away.

I've never lived in a morgue but I'm sure being in our house in those days was pretty much like doing so. Dave was being too bloody good to be true, studying for his entry exam for a Britsh university. The small brothers spent most of their time shut in their room playing games. Mother read, and read, and read . . . Rape and Pillage lay on the balcony bored out of their minds. There was still no sign of Richard, and if he had turned up I wouldn't have been allowed to talk to him anyway. Bad times. I was suffering severe sexual frustration. I mean, I had just spent the last few months rutting away like a stag with Judith, and now I was confined to nothing more than the thoughts in my head. Dave took to parading Jane up and down in front of me and then whipping her off for a quick one in my bunker. Of course my strategy had worked. He told me in minute detail how Jane had finally given up her troublesome piece of flesh and now couldn't get enough. The first time she saw me in my baggy shorts and with shorn locks and spectacles she just pointed and shrieked with laughter.

I couldn't even console myself by getting wrecked. The alcohol ban was strictly enforced: father had a tally board stuck on the outside of the fridge to keep track of the beers, and the bastard even lined off the whisky and gin bottles with a pen. I was desperate. And I still worried like hell about Judith and her pregnancy and who she was going to tell.

Then one day Dave came home from school with good news. 'You don't have to worry about Judith. She's gone back to England,' he said.

I felt anything but happy, and must have shown it.

'What's wrong with you?'

'I happen to like Judith very much.'

'Don't be stupid . . . You know what she was.'

'Yeah, sure, I know what she was, and I liked her for it.'

'You and every other male on Singapore. You don't even know that it was you, it could have been anyone who made her pregnant,' he said.

'That's true,' I had to admit.

He pulled a small bottle of whisky out of his school bag. 'Never mind all that shit anyway, get stuck into that bastard,' he said.

'Now that is good news,' I assured him, and we got quietly drunk in the bedroom.

'I thought you had reformed?' I said to Dave.

'Oh I have, but you can overdo things. Did I ever tell you that you look like a real prick?'

I threw a pillow at him. He knocked it aside.

'You should be very nice to me,' he said.

'Why?'

'I'm in the position of being able to do you a considerable favour.'

'And what would that be?'

He grinned.

'What about a favour called Carol?'

'Jesus, you're joking . . . '

'I'm not. She'd like to see you again. I could bring her over with Jane one night and smuggle them into the bedroom through the window.'

'In the house?' I shook my head. 'It would never work!'

'Why not?' he asked.

'Have you ever heard that Carol? I'm not kidding, she shouts her head off as soon as you touch her. Mother would hear her and her bloody "Fire!" from the other side of the island.'

'There's a school dance next week, you could come over to that . . . ' he suggested.

'Do you seriously think that I am going to a school dance looking like this?' I asked.

He shook his head, 'No, you do look a right dickhead.'

'Thanks, you black-eyed bastard.'

'I know. I'll get her over this Saturday. Mother and father

147

will be shopping on Singapore. You could meet her on the beach as if by accident.'

We shook hands and threw the last of the whisky down our throats.

Could I wait for Saturday to come around? Could I hell! I was like a wound-up spring just waiting to go off.

As soon as the parents had departed I ripped the disgusting clothes off, threw the glasses into a corner, found an old pair of shorts and raced down to the beach. On the way down I realised something was wrong. The dogs. Rape and Pillage were not there. They would never miss a run down to the beach. Never. I stopped and looked for them and whistled. Nothing. That was funny, very funny. I decided to look for them afterwards. Carol would probably moan if they were there anyway.

She was sat on a rock, facing out to sea, with her back to me.

'Hi,' I said.

She turned around, 'Holy smoke!' she laughed. 'What happened to you?'

'Is it that bad?' I asked.

'Yeah, it's that bad. I can't make up my mind whether I prefer you dirty and long-haired or clean and bald,' she answered.

'I don't have a lot of choice,' I said.

'No, you were much better with long hair and dirt, even if you did stink. It was sort of an animal smell,' she said.

I sat down with her. She pointed to the raft bobbing in the sea.

'A lot's happened since that night.'

'And most of it bad,' I said.

'You only have yourself to blame for that.'

'Yeah, I know.'

She looked at me for ages.

'You know what?' she said eventually.

'No, I don't know what.'

'I came over here because I wanted to do it with you again,' she said.

'And . . . '

'And I don't want to do it with you now.'

'Oh,' I said.

'They have finally crushed you, haven't they? Look at you, such a sweet little boy.'

I stared at the water.

'You know why I liked you, and wanted you . . . Not just me, all the others as well: Jane, Maria, Judith, Carol, all of them. Do you know why?' she asked.

I shook my head, still staring out over the water.

'Because you were wild, mad, crazy, like an animal. You did just what you bloody well wanted to do. You never let anyone tell you what to do. You got expelled from school for nearly killing Mr Perfect, you screwed who you liked, you screwed me on the raft with Maria waiting for you on the beach, and you would have screwed my sister as well, the same night, if you could have. You said fuck it to everything and everyone . . . And now look at you. Pathetic! In the end you are just the same as the rest of us. When you know it's coming to an end you conform like a good little boy. You are terrified of England and the real world. You are a coward, a liar and a cheat!'

She picked her stuff up off the rock and walked off without a backward glance. I stared out at the sea and little salt tears ran out of my eyes and dribbled down my cheeks, but I didn't sob. If you had been stood behind me you wouldn't have known that I was crying. I didn't cry. Oh no. I was too bloody tough.

She hit me harder than anybody else had ever hit me in my whole life. You couldn't make me cry with fists, but the plain ordinary truth crippled me.

Back at the house I found Rape and Pillage stretched out on the balcony in their usual sleeping place, and had to laugh at the lazy bastards . . . Until I noticed the flies buzzing around them in a swarm.

'Jesus!'

I prayed as I bent down by them, a prayer and not a curse. Their jaws hung open and a rancid green liquid had dribbled out and pooled on the floor by their heads. They were both stone dead. This time I did sob. The Malays had been trying to poison them or give them boiled eggs full of pins for years, but I had taught them not to take stuff off strangers or eat anything they found. I couldn't believe they had disobeyed a rule. That was something they had never done before. Never. It was impossible.

Then I heard a funny scratchy sound and looked up. What I saw made me want to pray again, but I was too petrified to speak. A massive, pure black king cobra was swaying to and fro right in front of me, its evil hood flared, its mouth open showing the pinky flesh and gleaming biting fangs. Richard had been looking for a pure black king cobra for years – their skin was worth a fortune . . . But I wasn't at all happy about finding this one.

I looked into the bastard's eyes and could see a black promise of forever glinting in there. If I so much as blinked an eyelid the monster would explode in a hissing flash. I thought: OK God, you've taken away everything I had – Richard, Rape, Pillage, Judith, Maria, Jane, Carol. Now you only have to clear up this last piece of debris and you can go to bed. Go on, do it! What the hell!

As if the cobra had heard me, it lunged suddenly forwards and I thought, This is it. But at the last moment it reared backwards again and swivelled its flat, ugly head slightly to one side, as though something else had caught its attention but it was still reluctant to take its eyes off me. Moving my head as slowly as I could I looked. Christ! It was Shitbag. He was frozen to the spot, exactly where he had landed after jumping out of the dining-room door on his way for a piss outside. He could have been carved from stone, one front paw raised in front of him as if he was about to move and the rest of his body frozen in mid-stride. Obviously he'd seen the king cobra. His big green eyes were focussed on me. His lower jaw opened so slow you'd have thought he was a puppet and he said, 'Meeoowwww?'

I know what he said. He said: 'What the hell is this? Do I go forwards or do I go back?'

I wanted to say, 'Shitbag, you back out of here, nice and slow, and everything will be all right.' But I couldn't say anything.

Another minute went by and the sweat was running into my eyes and I knew I would have to move soon. I watched Shitbag's eyes. They moved off my head and played over the bodies of Rape and Pillage, then wandered coolly over to the rearing form of the snake. The cobra spat out a furious hiss, and Shitbag suddenly started walking like someone had just wound him up and put him on the floor. His hips swung in a peculiar manner which I'd never seen before, his ears were low and his tail was bushed up to three times its normal size. He sauntered along, coming directly between the cobra and me. Jesus, I thought, what the hell are you doing. Shitbag!

Then the snake went for him. Its head shot forward with the speed of a bolt of electricity, fangs reaching out for his fur like a double-headed steel arrow of poison. But Shitbag was quicker. Shitbag was so damned quick that I couldn't even see what he did, but there he was hanging onto the back of that cobra's head by his teeth. The cobra went into parox-ysms of spitting fury, thrashing its head against the ground and the walls – *Whack! Whack!* – but Shitbag held on for grim death. They rolled across the floor, the snake's body pound-ing and thrashing at Shitbag, but he didn't let go. Venom poured out of the bastard's mouth and spattered the walls. In Shitbag's eyes there was a look of absolute madness . . . and victory. The snake's mad thrashing slowed down into no more than a spasmodic twitch and wriggle. Then it stopped altogether and Shitbag spat the head out of his mouth and looked at me with his big green eyes.

'Shit, Shitbag!' I said. 'Didn't anyone ever tell you that cats do not fight with cobras?'

His lower jaw fell open and he said, 'Meeooww.'

I know what he said. He said: 'Well, I'm no ordinary cat as you can see, and this is in fact the third snake I have beaten the living shit out of. Now, if you'd be good enough to open the fridge door for me, I could murder a beer, and then I'd like a little sleep in there.'

I walked over to look at the snake, but Shitbag growled low in his throat and bent over the body.

'OK, OK, it's your body,' I told him.

'Meeooww.'

'Oh, I think that's unfair, Shitbag. They were very good dogs in their time and I'm sure they did try their best. But that was one hell of a snake!'

'Meeooww!' he confirmed.

I went into the kitchen, ripped father's tally off the fridge door, got two beers out, opened one – Shitbag came hurtling in, he could hear a beer can open at fifty paces – and poured it into his saucer. I left the fridge door open for him and took the other beer outside. A little tableau of death was spread out on the balcony.

I wasn't crying any more. It was all over, as simple as that. The final earthquake had destroyed my paradise, forever and forever. Shitbag had shown me what Richard had taught me and I had almost forgotten. Let the bastards come up to the limit, but the minute they step over it, kill them. Just like Shitbag killed the cobra.

I dragged the bodies of Rape and Pillage out into the garden and, under the shade of the banana plants where Jane had introduced herself, I started digging a big hole. Shitbag sat and watched me. I got us two more beers.

Father and mother arrived back from their Singapore shopping expedition.

'You've been drinking!' he shouted at me, waving his discarded tally sheet when he found me in the garden.

'Go to hell!' I said, and carried on digging the hole.

'Don't talk to me like that! And what the bloody hell do you think you're doing?'

'I am burying my dogs, OK?'

'Oh,' he said, and peered at the two bodies.

'I knew I must have learned that from someone,' I said.

'What?'

'To say that word "Oh" at important moments,' I told him.

'Oh,' he said again.

'Christ!' I swore, and carried on digging.

Mother came out.

'What happened?' she asked, dismayed. She actually liked the dogs.

I picked up the body of the cobra and threw it at their feet. They jumped back.

'That's what happened. But Shitbag got the bastard back, didn't you Shitbag?'

'Meeeooww,' he said.

While they were still staring at the bodies, I went in and got two more beers. Father watched in astonishment as I poured one into a bowl for Shitbag.

'That's my bloody beer and you're forbidden to drink here anyway. If you don't put that down right now you're on your way home, right now, on a VC10 back to England!' he shouted.

I drunk the beer down in one go and threw the empty can into the hole. I thought Rape and Pillage would appreciate the gesture . . .

'I want to go, right now. There is nothing left for me here, nothing,' I told him.

'Right,' he said and rushed off.

Mother looked at me, shook her head and was about to say something. But I got there first.

'No, don't say anything, mother. This is no longer my island and I want out.'

She went inside and I buried Rape and Pillage and patted Shitbag on the head.

'Bye old mate. I never realised what a good little Shitbag you were. We should have spent more time together.'

'Meeooww,' he said.

Dave was cut up about the dogs but we didn't get an awful lot of time to discuss such things. Father had me on a flight that evening, as an unaccompanied minor. On the jetty Dave and I shook hands and I said, 'Look after Shitbag. That is one good animal.'

'You look after yourself, although my opinion is that you are the maddest, baddest bastard that ever drew breath as a boy and you won't live to see twenty,' he said, with his black eyes shining.

'We shall see, we shall see,' I told him, and got on the boat with a small travel bag and a hell of a lot of ghosts.

* * *

And all that passed in between? Between then and now? Between then, when I was fleeing from ghosts, and now, when I'm running away from myself and that mad toad the Boss and a nervous breakdown back in the land of Mr Lee Kuan Facking Yew? Things didn't get any better: I got my skull smashed in by some drunken whore in the Spurs Nightclub in Cape Town, caught syphilis in San Juan, was stabbed in Miami, jailed in Bermuda, had a plane crash in the one-eyed Pacific, got poisoned by a mad one-eyed cook in the Indian Ocean. And so on.

And I never got around to the Boss. Probably a good thing. I honestly think I have got myself together now. I will walk out of this hotel room and take a flight to somewhere. If I had started on about the Boss, I might have taken that trip out of the window. We'll save that one till my sanity is reconfirmed.

When I look out of the window of my twenty-fourth-storey hotel room, I can see the taxis passing by on their way to the airport. Twenty-two years ago I was probably looking up at this very window wondering where I was going to go and what I was going to do.

Not much has changed.